Reparations
MAZE

PHILIP WYETH

Also by this author:
Reparations USA
Reparations Mind
Reparations Core
Chasing the Best Days
Hot Ash and the Oasis Defect

Cover design by Philip Wyeth.

www.philipwyeth.com

CONTENTS

1. PEACEKEEPERS

The headwaiter shuffled over to a small table near the back wall, carrying in each hand an enormous steaming plate of spaghetti. He set these down in front of two men, being careful not to splash any of the red sauce onto them or his own white formal shirt. He bowed and moved away.

One of the men, a middle-aged Caucasian with sparse hair and a black-dyed beard, gently nudged his plate aside and consulted a pocket flip pad. He made a mark on one line of the page, then looked up.

"So, that takes care of robberies. You ready to talk fights?"

The other man chuckled. A grizzled Afrigro-American with buzz-shaved head, he still possessed an athletic build despite his advancing age. He said, "The ones on camera… or off?"

"Well, that depends. How many are, uh, Certified Historical Events that got our friends in law enforcement involved?"

"Come on, Michelangelo. You know I can't keep track of all that. Just too many Domination Events taking place between our people, you feel me?"

"Of course." As he took a bite of his meal, Michelangelo said, "But that's alright. Let's not lose the forest for the trees. 'Cause Duke, you and me, we do some good business together. Sometimes you leave the table up, sometimes you're down. But mostly it all evens out. So please, eat your food. We'll square this in good time."

"True that, my friend."

Over the next half hour, Duke and Michelangelo haggled over the handwritten lists that ran down each of their notepads. The plates were cleared away, then coffee and port arrived. Finally, Michelangelo scribbled something onto a cocktail napkin and handed it to Duke.

The black man closed his eyes drowsily and shrugged his shoulders. "Okay. So I walk out of here a winner this month."

Michelangelo snapped his fingers. A skinny teenager who had been standing in the shadows near the kitchen now approached. A few words were exchanged quietly, and then the boy walked through the empty restaurant out into the street.

"An extra measure of precaution," Michelangelo said with a wave. "To keep our, uh, freelance conflict resolution service a private matter."

Duke nodded. He tapped a fingernail against his glass of port. "Well, I'll take this type of service over standing in line at the HRA any day of the week."

The men laughed together heartily. A moment later, Michelangelo adjusted himself in his seat and wiped the corner of his mouth with a cloth napkin.

"So tell me," he said, "how's the family? Everyone

good?"

"Oh, you know how it is. They're fine. Got no time or patience for the man who holds it all together… But they're good, doing real good."

Michelangelo smiled softly. "Everybody thinks that this is easy. Sitting around in fancy suits, eating and drinking, just a couple of guys shooting the breeze, right? If only they could see below the surface!"

"Mm," Duke grumbled. "Don't even offer to trade places with me for an hour. 'Cause if I got *one taste* of that weight off my shoulders, I'd probably never let 'em put it back."

"Absolutely. People take what we do for granted. Keeping peace in the streets—relatively speaking, of course. But more importantly, limiting each neighborhood's exposure to the surveillance pipeline."

"That's it! We keep all their Debit Scores down, for Christ's sake. Keep the tension from spilling over into chaos, so they can go about their lives. But oh, 'Papa Duke goin' off on one of his pub crawls again.' My foot! I'm the person cleaning up all *their* vomit."

Just then the front door of the restaurant opened and the lanky young man returned. He pulled a frosted plastic tube out of his inside jean jacket pocket and handed it to Michelangelo without a word, then moved away to his spot in the shadows.

Michelangelo gave the green-capped container a little shake and held it out over the table. "Here ya go, count the coins if you want. You're the big winner."

"Unfortunately my jackpot is destined to be short-lived," Duke said with a chuckle as he received the bullion. He stowed it inside his blazer. "Next stop for me is Rabbi Lovitz. I got to hustle over there before sundown. I swear, the knockout game ain't no game when it comes to these here private payouts, no sir."

Michelangelo rose to escort Duke to the exit. "Maintenance work is rarely glamorous. But why should everything that happens be the entire world's business? So, we settle these trifling debts our way. Wipe the hard drives, seal the records before—"

Duke rapped a knuckle against the doorframe twice. "Before MARVIN drops in for a visit. Mm-hmm. See you next time, *compadre*. And thanks for the supper!"

"Anytime. You have yourself a nice New Year… *Il Duce*."

The men shook hands and Duke stepped out into the cool gray day.

2. EQUITUS

Security was tight at the Kennedy Center on Saturday evening. Patrons found themselves required to pass through a limited number of entryways before gaining access to the famed theater's bright red carpeting. Once inside, they encountered members of the Secret Service who were posted throughout the venue.

Because tonight, in their final public appearance of the year, the President and First Man would attend the Noah Rafferty play *Equitus*.

A hush fell over the crowd. Heads turned and craned upward. There were murmurs, then loud applause erupted as Eileen Jeffries-Lao and husband Paul Jeffries entered their private box and came into view. She was wearing an elegant navy blue dress that sparkled from a thousand different points.

The couple waved graciously, then motioned for people to retake their seats. Several minutes later, the theater lights faded out and the performance began.

Equitus was the shocking story of a troubled young man who live-streamed charitable acts by day, but later committed hate crimes in fits of amnesic rage. A love triangle involving his employer's Affirmative Action hire and a woman he'd known in high school propelled him inexorably toward a psychotic break—or perhaps the breakthrough that would change his fortunes forever.

"Ridiculous!" Eileen heard Paul snort late in the first act. He was seated to her left, his right leg crossed over top and body leaning away.

"What now?" she whispered.

Paul waved a hand toward the stage. "More sex, that's what!"

"But darling, these two have been dancing around the tension ever since they drove to the soup kitchen together."

"Eh, maybe. I thought this kid was finally going to look in the mirror. Now *another* roll in the hay to solve his problems?"

Eileen cast a sideways glance at Paul in the faint light. She said, "Isn't that how you've always gone about it?"

Paul's leg slid down and he turned toward her, mouth agape for a moment. Then he smiled, saying, "Don't be resentful just because you showed up late to the party."

"What is *that* supposed to mean?"

"Please. People talk. Word gets around. I'm aware of certain… work friendships over at Sixteen Hundred Pennsylvania Avenue."

Eileen Jeffries-Lao felt a shiver run across the surface of her body. The ongoing affair with her chief of staff, which she had tried to keep a secret from everyone… Who else knew?

"I…" Her voice trailed off. Down below, the hay-rolling actress's father was in a huff about something.

She felt a pat on her knee.

"It's alright," Paul said. "Everyone's got to play their role up on stage. You got your 'four more years.' So, whatever it takes to sustain you across the finish line, I understand."

Eileen cocked her head at an angle. "But still, you're jealous? Or mad?"

He chuckled, saying, "You've no idea the types of indignities that the husband of a pioneering female politician must endure. Who you engage in pillow talk with is the least of my troubles—especially at this late hour in your career."

"Oh. So you're watching the clock, now that you believe my stock is done rising?"

"Possib*ly*. Although I don't imagine either one of us expects to retire to some palatial estate together and pass the years quietly."

Eileen reached for her wine glass, while her mind envisioned a distant fork in the road. On one path, that idyllic retirement where she would play grandmother to her daughter's children. On the other, working even more feverishly with the international power brokers who were secretly engineering the great space project that would send humanity to the stars.

But an arduous second term as president lay between her and that day in 2033. All the travel, the speeches, and cagey political decisions that would be laid at her feet—and upon her legacy. Perhaps even the quietly proposed scaling back of the domestic Reparations program. Cord cutting done only for the greater good, of course…

"Ah, the gears are turning now," she heard Paul say. He frowned and added, "I do hope you aren't planning to have me offed. No need, my dear. I'll continue to stay out of your way. But always ready to keep up appearances! Oh yes, you can certainly rely on this old soldier!"

Eileen watched as he rattled the ice cubes inside his whiskey glass and drank. The First Man in that moment looked stoic, and yet so very small. He had paid a tremendous price in hitching his wagon to her—a WASP marrying a second-generation Chinese immigrant, then playing second fiddle throughout the course of her career. And with the Historical Reparations Administration serving as the capstone of her presidency, perhaps there was something cruelly poetic about his having to attend so many events where he stood in as the symbolic fall guy.

Liquor and young ladies were the balm for Paul's frustration, which Eileen had at least understood if not quite forgiven. But now with Tony Rizzuto as her own guilty pleasure, the drug to help endure the strain of it all... Not only was she no better than her philandering husband, he seemed to have cultivated an artful veneer that masked his disappointments and imperfections.

As for herself, bearing the weight of so many critical responsibilities had apparently left her susceptible to one of the little vices that so often ensnared the types of people she looked down upon.

Eileen reached out and clinked her glass against Paul's tumbler. "Thank you. Maybe we *will* have something to talk about when all is said and done."

"Shh," he said. "I think someone else is about to have sex now. Or maybe get assaulted. You never can tell with these modern plays..."

The president turned her eyes back toward the stage.

3. THE NICE PLACE

"All in a day's work, my friends."

The Reverend Matthias G. Witherspoon tugged at the zipper of his jacket, then used the long grabber tool he was carrying to snatch a mangled plastic food container out of the grass.

"Yes sir, you kids are getting a real taste of what it's like to help your community."

Surrounding him were half a dozen boys, each carrying a thick orange plastic bag and wearing work gloves. Every so often one of them would reach down and pick up a piece of trash.

"Don't let me catch you dawdling now," Witherspoon added. "It ain't *that* cold out today. And the alternative—well, y'all already know a thing or two about juvenile hall."

"It ain't so bad in there," one of the boys said. Matthias gauged him to be about ten years old. "Got TVs, hoops…"

"That's what they want you to think, Geoffrey. Make you feel comfy behind bars. Not so you'll reconsider your mischievous ways, neither. Nah, they gettin' you used to the idea of spending your life inside a cage."

The group arrived at a residential intersection. Reverend Witherspoon said, "Well, which side looks worse off, left or right?"

"Left," one boy said.

"Right!" another declared.

"Let's split up," a third offered.

Matthias said, "No way. We operate as a team, watch each other's backs. Need to do a thorough job out here for these folks, too. Why? Because everybody wants to go to the nice place—instead of doing the work to make *a place nice*. So many people got a chip on their shoulder, and an excuse on the tip of their tongue. And when they put their hand out, that completes the Holy Trinity of Failure. But not me, for I choose to take pride in this town. Anyhow, I say we go to the right. Ten minutes, we'll pass the truck, get a sip of water and swap out any bags that are full. So come on."

The clean-up crew slowly made its way along a quiet street that was flanked on one side by a warped chain-link fence. As they retrieved crushed cans and discarded toys and the occasional piece of wet clothing, Reverend Witherspoon felt a wave of contentment warm him from within. Initially his return from sabbatical had not gone smoothly, but now everything seemed to have worked out.

He brokered a peace deal between the warring factions inside his church—those who attended primarily for social reasons versus the parishioners inspired by his fiery October sermon to take Christianity, and life itself, more seriously. A balanced schedule of events, patient discussions with all aggrieved parties, and a commitment to turn frustration into meaningful action had helped mend the congregation's fractures.

Litter removal was just one of the many activities he hoped would not simply engage with the local community, but help to unify and revitalize it. He felt that these kids here with him today were much too young to get caught up in the criminal justice system, let alone the street life, and so Matthias took great pride in this mentorship opportunity.

"Y'all are some good dudes," he said, exhaling into the cool air. "Just got too much free time for all that energy. You don't realize what I'm about to explain, 'cause how could you know? But truth is, all them cops and judges and lawyers, they *want* y'all to act stupid and break the law."

He heard a scraping sound and then watched as a glass bottle went bouncing down the street. Nicholas, who had kicked it, said, "I think you lyin'. That don't make no sense!"

"Oh, we got a skeptic here. That's fine. So tell me, Mister Nick, how am I wrong?"

The boy, only eleven but already capable of a fierce scowl, said, "They ain't like… construction workers, who come in and make something new. Nah, all they do is the cleanup."

"That's riiiight," Matthias said. "And speaking of which, don't you forget to pick up that bottle you thought was a soccer ball… But let's get into it, and I hope you other boys is listening, 'cause your friend Nicholas might teach you something here."

"Yeah, yeah," the other boys said. They were starting to get tired, Matthias noticed, lazily kicking at the plastic bags as they moved along.

"So check this out. A super-secret life lesson

courtesy of the Reverend Witherspoon himself. And free of charge. You don't even have to put on your Sunday best and step inside the church. Now look across the way there. Y'all see that house? Nice place. Up above, power lines on the poles. Pipes under the road too. I bet there'll be a couple cars pulling into that drive end of the day. That all costs money."

Geoffrey said, "Cash money! Mm-hmm."

Matthias paused to grab a soda cup with his claw. "Yep. Money, cooperation, all that community stuff I been talkin' about. So… Okay, sometimes in the kitchen you spill or break an egg on the floor, right? Accidents happen, but you still get to eat your meal."

"When are *we* gonna eat," Matthias heard a voice whine softly from behind.

"The problem comes when certain people make it they life habit to always be that broken egg. The mess! Society says, 'What can we do?! We tryin' to move forward, but this crew always settin' us back a step.' So what you think now, Nicholas?"

"They going to kill us?" the boy asked.

"Ha! They *wish!* So don't give 'em no ideas. But no. What they do is flip the mess into their own favor. They already set the world up for makin' money, so now that's what they do with lawbreakers. From the policeman to the attorney's secretary on down, they *all* cashin' in on folks who play the fool. And it's *better* than a meal, because that you only get to eat one time. But a repeat offender, my God! That's like in pinball when your ball gets stuck up at the top. Bouncin' and bangin' all around those bumpers racking up points, and you don't even have to do a thing. Are you startin' to feel me, fellas? Anyone?"

Geoffrey said, "So, like, where they get the money from? Who pay them?"

"Good question, young man. Very astute. The answer is, the taxpayers. All the other people who live here in town. And for them, it's worth it. They're happy to pay their neighbor the judge to keep the ruffians off the street. Now lemme get real with y'all. How many of you know someone been locked up a bunch of times?"

Matthias paused to make a count of hands, but before he could continue, Nicholas said, "And you think that gonna be us too? That we next?"

The reverend exhaled heavily. "Look here. I don't believe any one of you got malice in your heart. Truly. But the system don't care—it can't *see* that part. All those vultures see is another black boy shoplifting from the convenience store. All they see is y'all voluntarily posting videos of you and your friends gangin' up and beatin' on somebody. And Lord of Mercy, that is why I'm trying to intervene on your behalf! To talk some sense into you before you really go too far, and they lock you up and throw away the key. Because the coppers and all them, their lives are totally set up. Sittin' on their butts until fresh criminals come along and give 'em something to do. So tell me, you still wanna step in their trap, now that you know it's there?"

The boys had stopped walking. There was the occasional sound of crinkling plastic as one of them adjusted his weight. A police cruiser rounded the corner at the end of the block, and Reverend Witherspoon waved at the white officer as the car rolled past.

"See?" Matthias said. "Someone's always keepin' an eye out."

A boy named Ismael dropped his bag and said sadly, "What we supposed to do? If they just waitin' for us to mess up... Sound like we always gonna get caught in the mix."

"My friend, I do not know. But stick with old Matthias and we'll try to figure it out. At least now you know something you didn't before this morning. So let's wrap it up for today, get out those sandwiches, and I'll log in your hours. Few more sessions with me, not only will this town be looking more beautiful than ever, maybe we can cook up a plan to keep you fine youngsters out of the legal system's teeth. 'Cause believe you me, even when you done *nothing* wrong, they'll still take a chunk out of you. Consider for example the former Mrs. Witherspoon, who at present is living in a mighty fine house that was paid for by yours truly…"

4. THE MOST BEAUTIFUL BOW

It was all so bittersweet. What with everything happening down in DC for President Jeffries-Lao's second inauguration, and Kate Donohugh being completely out of the mix.

Weeks ago she had stepped down from her position as HRA liaison working at the White House's behest. Packed up her belongings from her parents' house in Arlington and returned to Brooklyn, where she resumed her duties at the HRA megabranch in Newark.

But that wasn't all. She had a little secret no one else knew about. One that, if it came to fruition, would change everything and put the most beautiful bow on what had been the wildest year of her life.

She was pregnant. It was only the first month, however. Far too early to tell anyone, let alone make plans or think hopeful thoughts which might reverberate for the rest of her life.

She needed to stick to her normal routine—walk the dogs, work diligently, and keep riding the wave of reconciliation she'd been on with her husband Chris ever since returning from a disastrous overseas HRA work trip in November.

But now, while tidying up the apartment after a small New Year's Eve party, Kate pictured the living room floor as it might look when littered with brightly colored children's toys. Her mind started to helicopter up into the clouds as one pleasant future vision triggered another, and soon she was dancing through fantasy land.

It might have been the first time in her life that she truly wanted something just for herself. Because through the years, something *external* had always pushed her toward whatever she did. Go to college not simply to learn, but to get a good job. Join a volunteer organization to save this endangered species, or protect that marginalized group. And finally, work for the HRA to *avenge* the past.

She held her breath for a moment, suspecting that she had stumbled upon another layer that was hidden beneath this role of playing helper. Something negative, angry... Something that thought in zero-sum terms, rather than of building on top of what good was already there.

Kate looked down at her body, thinking, *But this is different. This little thing is completely vulnerable. Later, when she comes out, her skull will be soft, her neck too weak to support the head. No words, no thoughts. Just needs—for milk, for warmth, to know she's still protected and safe after leaving my body.*

And then what? Kate would teach this baby words... in order to tell her how privileged she was? To start planting those seeds of doubt and self-recrimination before she'd even taken her first steps? Make this child question herself, rather than blossom confidently?

Kate vowed that she would not allow her daughter's mind to be influenced at such a young age. There had to be another way to teach empathy without putting a person's own foundations at risk.

There's a new life inside of me. I must protect her. She is mine! *My responsibility. She does* not *belong to the world...*

But it was still so very early. Any number of things could go wrong. Then she would be right back where she started—but also carrying heartache instead of a child...

Kate set her cleaning supplies down and closed her eyes. She took a moment to remind herself how blessed she already was. With health after a breast cancer scare that had mercifully only required a brief series of radiation treatments. Blessed with family and friends. A nice apartment. Coworkers who adored her.

And then there was the job itself. Assistant regional manager for the Historical Reparations Administration. Source of both satisfaction and strain. Career fulfillment after nearly a decade of working with activist groups.

Would she really go back to work when her maternity leave ended? After so many years spent battling on the front lines of progressive politics, suddenly she saw how tempting it would be to check out completely.

But logistics were a very real consideration. Chris ran a small one-person tech design business. While his clients did keep him busy, it was really Kate's government salary and gold-standard benefits package that fueled their household. He would most certainly have to take a real job if she decided to be a stay-at-home mom...

Kate shook her head. The instant that thought

crossed her mind, she knew how cruel it was. Implying that what Chris did wasn't substantial, or meaningful in its own way. Belittling sideswipes like that were what had ground him down and put their marriage on the rocks just two months ago.

She would have to keep working on herself. Cut negative thoughts off at the pass. Respect her husband and their special bond. She knew in her heart they could navigate around whatever new challenges lay ahead. Because it was all worth it. And would be ever more so, if their family grew to three.

Plus the two Corgis, of course.

5. A WIN-WIN

"Well? What do ya think?"

Clyde Jenkins turned away from the TV screen and glanced at Eddie Pryor. The man's eyes were bulging in anticipation of what Clyde would say about this other rapper who was being pitched to team up with on a new song.

"It's kinda weird, to be honest," he replied.

"I know, I know," Eddie said. "But it's unprecedented what this guy does—and *did*."

Clyde wondered, *How can Eddie act so smart, but then sometimes he seems really dumb?*

He was recalling how this Hollywood mogul had suggested—no, insisted that Clyde's family fly out and visit Los Angeles. His mother Dawna, sister Myra and her boyfriend Octavius, plus his young niece and nephew all got the royal treatment around town during the Holy Holidays. But Clyde now suspected that this invitation hadn't come strictly from the goodness of Eddie's heart. More likely, it was a calculated move to prevent Clyde from having second thoughts about their freshly inked deal, had he taken a trip back home to Newark.

That was the man's smart side. But the proposed pairing with this other artist did not seem to make any sense.

DJ Low Bought started out as just another singer who had grown up poor, before catching a wave of success with some mix tapes under his first stage name, MC Nyte Nyte Nine. But a couple years back *something* happened—a car accident while not wearing his seat belt, or maybe resisting arrest during a drug-fueled freak out. The end result was that a portion of his brain had been surgically removed. And then, contrary to what all common wisdom suggested, he'd had *even more* success under his new moniker.

But all Clyde saw was a man who had taken mumble rap to a ridiculous new level of spectacle— complete with diamond-crusted scooter, bandana-print bib, and an 18-karat-gold drool pan in the lap. While the circular and rhythmic sounds that emitted from DJ Low Bought's quavering mouth were in fact hypnotic, Clyde could not fathom why Eddie Pryor wanted this guy of all people to be a part of his next song.

Clyde said, "There's got to be other dudes, or girls, who rap about the same kind of stuff as me. Because Low, he just makes crazy noises. So… I don't see what you see. Sorry, man."

Eddie sighed and rolled his chair away from the desk. They were in his private office which overlooked Hollywood toward the south. "Your concerns are understandable. And Clyde, I'm always happy to hold your hand and explain things to you. God knows, at least you *listen* and try to make the right decision."

A smile transformed Eddie's face. He said, "So here's the plan. Many people believe that you, Clyde

Jenkins, have the Midas Touch, right? Turning everything into gold—or platinum, as the case may be, hehe. So… I'm gonna let you in on a little secret. And don't you *dare* spill the beans. Otherwise someone, who's probably much taller than me, will come and *mess you up!*"

"Jesus, Eddie!" Clyde cried. "What the hell is it?"

"I'm saying that DJ Low has been faking it the whole time! Do you *really* think someone with a half-empty skull can rap to a beat that's in nine-sixteenths time?! Come on, it was a gimmick—one that took on a life of its own. Who knows, maybe it started out as a bet to see what people were willing to go along with."

"Oh," Clyde said quietly. "So if I'm serious and he been playin'… How do we meet up?"

"Exactly! Because, Mister Midas, *you* are going to use your superpower of truth to reveal and heal him. First, we'll get a whole religious theme going. Then in the middle of the song, you—the wise man of integrity —will call out this sinner who's been hiding in plain sight.

"The extras wheel him up to the stage, arms twitching, lips babbling, while you deliver a sermon about how it's time to put an end to lies in the name of purity and goodness. Slowly he rises up… a rejuvenated man with his faculties restored… and together you guys dish out some great rhymes. The end!"

Eddie gave a self-satisfied smile. By now even Clyde was laughing along. He said, "Oh, okay. This is all really weird, but kind of fun too, I guess. What do you think will happen when people find out it was all a game?"

"Who the hell knows? But that's part of the thrill. Phase three of Low's career could be the biggest yet—

or maybe someone whacks him with a lead pipe and he really does end up a vegetable. Ha!"

Clyde thought for a moment. Then he said, "So DJ Low already been acting like that for two years. How long was it supposed to go on? Or did you already know when you were gonna break his cover?"

"Well, Clyde, we're always drawing up new storylines here in the command center. Kind of like pro wrestling, except it's artists and celebrities. Their projects, as well as their private lives. My guess is someone here on staff toyed with the idea that you, DJ Clydoscope, might be a good fit to pull back the curtain. So we ran some models in our system and yeah, it all looked good. I mean, picture it. You arrive on the LA scene dropping this earthquake of a hit single—and finally Low can go back to walking around in public without a diaper on. I'd say that's a win-win!"

Clyde left his chair and walked to the window. A few months ago, he would have bristled at being part of such a silly song. But he was in it for the long haul now. He intended to dazzle the world for years— decades even!—and if the price was a few compromises along the way, so be it.

He turned back toward the office and said, "Alright, Eddie. I'm in. Guess I better get fitted for my preacher's robe then, huh?"

"That's the spirit," Pryor beamed. "The Holy Spirit!"

They high-fived and retook their seats.

6. RIPPLES OF TRAUMA

He was lost in a violent swirl of nightmares. Faces from the past painted in ghastly colors morphed into abstract shapes, then another horrid memory entered the frame. His soul howled for relief from these ancient torments as they gushed through the breached dam which had held them back for decades.

Time had ceased to exist. There were moments of calm reprieve, then a cool liquid rush sent his psyche hurtling back into the chaotic torrent once more. He thrashed frantically against pain... fear... doubt... the hundred soul-killing paths which could send a human mind into the bleakest corners of despair.

As these hellish waters slowly receded for the last time, Scott Cullen sensed that his captors were ending the torture simply because they had broken him to the point that there was nothing more to take. Beyond the confession of any worldly crimes, perhaps he had also admitted to some vulnerability or hideous truth that was still unknown to his conscious mind. And it was the ultimate motivator, the secret fuel which had driven him so hard and so far throughout his life.

Now, as he began the slow process of withdrawal from these drugs—regaining his senses and rebuilding his strength—Scott remained at the mercy of the federal government and the case its lawyers were surely building against him.

Decades in prison seemed a foregone conclusion. A treason conviction might bring the death penalty. What would become of the Church of Modestianity? What would his thousands of followers *do* if the Prescient One became the young religion's first martyr?

Scott wondered what he would say if he ever got another opportunity to speak to them. He couldn't pretend as if nothing had changed inside of himself, or preach confidently while hiding this raw spiritual gash beneath his cloak. No, he would have to dive back down, bring it into full focus, and then face it without fear.

As he fell into a quiet meditation, a scene from over twenty years prior flashed before his eyes. He was walking to school on a cold winter morning. Suddenly a car pulled up beside him. A female classmate he liked was being driven by her father. The man offered to take him the rest of the way. And Scott said no.

With his head drooping, he made that same lonely walk every day the rest of the year, when if he'd had the courage to do what his heart wanted, perhaps he would have kept carpooling with them, and maybe even become the girl's boyfriend—and then those years would not have been so crushingly hollow.

But instead, Scott Cullen kept to himself and mastered all the facets of computing that enabled him to design a video game which made him rich and famous while still in college. This obsessive drive to work in near-isolation... It was not simply dedication.

There was an obscure darkness compelling him to immerse into *projects*, the same way that political types devoted their lives to *causes*. And yet, self-denial for a higher purpose had been responsible for the game *Thor's Tablet* and later the timely Church of Modestianity...

It was all masks and evasions. Burying his pain beneath frantic efforts, but never able to outrun the latent damage. Like an engine with an oil leak, sapping his soul drop by drop back into the inevitable sinking feeling after every triumph.

But how long could a person be propelled toward heroic deeds by the ripples of trauma which emanated perhaps from early childhood, if not also through ancestral memory? A life without the capacity for joy, either because it had been stolen or crushed, was sure to inevitably crumble—no matter how successful it appeared before that fateful moment of collapse.

Scott pursued that elusive source of existential nausea from within the confines of his jail cell. Tried to unravel the paradox of how fatalism could be converted into *performance* over and over again. Sought the cause and memory of his original wound. But this mysterious final layer, and the residue of psychological destruction, remained shrouded...

He had been in agony for far too long. And now that he was on the cusp of losing everything he possessed in the outside world, Scott Cullen could no longer carry the sickening weight that kept him trapped within a prism of dread.

He stalked the corridors of his mind each day. Eliminating a culprit here. Staring down an old regret there. Walling off alleys and mazes that were infested with self-effacing negativity. On and on...

He trudged relentlessly through the worst

nightmares, the hazy sensations that suggested abuse, or paralyzing terror, or neglect, or humiliation, or betrayed trust… or simply his own faulty wiring.

A deceptively soothing voice offered him the promise of quiet sleep, if he would just give in to despondency. But he refused to let the pilot light of his soul be snuffed out—because if he survived this ultimate reckoning with a single *shred* of sanity, let alone goodwill…

Then surely Scott Cullen could rise once again, and emerge with grace in his heart.

7. OUTNUMBERED

Luis Ortega's schoolwork was laid out before him on a circular concrete picnic table in the courtyard of the LA City College campus. It was a pleasant sixty-five degrees and he was focused on an assignment for his electrical engineering class. He did not sense when the small group crept up and surrounded his table.

"Ay, you the Ortega kid?"

Luis looked up from his work. In front of him stood two guys and girl. Glancing over his shoulder, he saw that two others were hovering aggressively close.

"Uh, yeah," he said. "That's me. What do you guys need?"

"We just want to ask you a couple questions," a tall Latizo in black t-shirt and faded jeans said as he sat down across from Luis.

"Like what? School stuff?"

"Nah," the guy said with a laugh. "We's like, wondering why you think you're better 'n all of us?"

Luis nervously pulled his school materials closer, then said, "I don't even know who you are, man. How am I supposed—"

He felt a light slap from behind and his baseball cap fell down onto the table. "Listen to this fool!" a voice grunted. "Playin' like he dumb."

Luis looked down and readjusted his glasses. "So we're back in high school, is that it? You think because I'm little, you can just—"

"Shut your friggin' mouth!" the first guy snapped. "Naw, this got nothin' to do with school shit. This about you runnin' your mouth on TV, messin' with everybody's HRA flow."

"Oh." Luis saw for the first time the anger in these brown and black faces that surrounded him. He braced himself for the beating that might come if he said anything which provoked them further. "What do you want me to do?"

The Afrigro-American girl jammed her hands into her pockets and said, "You don't like gettin' paid, why not take yo' sorry ass back to Mexico?"

The group laughed and exchanged fist bumps, then crowded Luis even closer. The guy sitting on the bench raised his arms for silence.

"Look, Luis. I'm Latiz like you, so forget her." He smirked at the girl. "You can stay in LA, it's cool, amigo. But maybe you got to keep a lower profile, know what I'm sayin'? Think about the rest of us—we ain't as *privileged* as the other kids in your lawsuit. We got to eat too. So stay away from the cameras, 'cause we *do not* want to see your stupid face on the news no more!"

Luis smiled involuntarily. "You're kidding me, right? The *last* thing I wanted was attention. I'm trying to do my damn work for class, man. But no one will leave me alone—not even you!"

Quickly he grabbed the edge of the table, then pushed himself off the bench before the person behind him could grab his shoulders. He scurried toward some other students who were walking past, but they jumped back and scattered, so he ran over to another table and climbed up onto the surface.

"Is no one gonna help me?" he pleaded with panting breath. "Crap! I thought college meant no more gang stuff. What the hell, guys?"

Luis felt terror rise up from his shuddering heart. Dozens of students were staring at him maliciously. In that moment, he wasn't a fellow Minorican. He represented a threat to the way of life that Beneficiaries had gotten used to—and one of these days, they might want to do more than just chat.

He nearly vomited as he thought about his two cousins who had been beheaded by cartel members in Mexico a few years ago. His parents believed they had left all of that behind by moving to the United States...

Luis now watched as the intimidating group first trashed his belongings, then sauntered across the courtyard loudly. When he was sure that they were gone, he stepped down from the table and picked up his scattered possessions.

Today his friends from the HRA-defying legal petition seemed very far away. He didn't want to let them down by backing out of the whole thing, but none of them could protect him in his daily life, either. He was also mortified at the thought of telling his long-distance girlfriend Cristina about what had happened—and felt deep shame because he had not been able to stand up for himself when outnumbered.

He just wanted to be left in peace to live his life. As it was, he'd barely had the heart to endure any of what had befallen him in recent months. First the mandatory appearance on *DDM TV Live*, then fleeing the set during the chaos of the hacked broadcast. Going from fugitive to hero to advocate... and yet somehow, now he was seen as a villain.

The weight of the world was suffocating young Luis Ortega, and he didn't know how he would ever break free.

8. PROVING GROUNDS

"Here's the stuff. Jesus, what a nightmare…"

Nolan Simmons waved at the stacks of boxes piled six feet high which filled half of the small office space.

"You want us to go through it?" Jaden asked. He and his friend Harvell sometimes helped Nolan with maintenance and other grunt work to make extra cash.

"Nah," Nolan said. "Toss it."

"What is all of that though?"

"Just stuff that's accumulated over the years. Got moved from place to place. It's time to stop pretending I'll ever get around to dealing with it. Especially now that we need the space."

"Oh, okay. So take it all down to the dumpster? Or the donation place?"

"Hell no to both! I want you to load up the van and head over to the same spot I sent y'all after Quincy got pinched a year back. Remember that?"

Harvell spoke up for the first time. He said, "But those things Mister Q. had was hot. Or knock-offs, right? This shit here…" He kicked at the boxes. "Look like a bunch of junk."

Nolan said, "You ain't wrong. But it's still got to be dealt with properly. Lemme show you why."

He pulled a medium-sized moving box off the top and ripped open the flaps, then tossed the contents onto the floor as he rummaged through.

"What do we got in this one? A clock... Oven mitt... Aha! Some papers! Car loan documents. Small claims court crap. Copy of an old lease from 'twenty-three. Are you starting to catch on? This is my personal paper trail. And I don't want none of my business falling into the wrong scans."

"We got you, boss," Jaden said. "We'll take care of it. Uh... still want me to shoot pictures, like last time? I mean, I know it's your own stuff, but figured I'd ask."

"Definitely. Gimme proof that the past has gone... poof!"

Nolan left them alone with the hand truck to load up the elevator, and then trip by trip, remove the clutter from his life forever.

Tomorrow some potential video clients were scheduled to check out the one-on-one interview setup in the soundstage down the hall, so all of the miscellaneous studio gear that was lying around needed to be moved into the space that the guys were clearing out. Nolan began organizing those items so that everything could be filed away neatly for future ease of access.

A few minutes later, however, there was a knock at the door. He glanced over his shoulder and saw Harvell standing there with a cardboard box in his hands.

"What's up?" he asked. "Is there a problem?"

"I know you said to throw everything away," Harvell began. "But I thought you might want to check this one out first."

Nolan set down the cables he was untangling and approached. "Why you say that?"

"Look." Harvell pointed at the words written in thick black marker across the top. "It's your Army things. Figured you'd probably want to keep some of 'em."

"I'll be damned."

Nolan took hold of the box and added, "Good looking out, Harv. Anything else catch your eye, you can maybe set it aside."

"No doubt, will do."

Nolan used a utility knife to carefully slice the box top open. He reached inside and felt his mind fall into a vortex of memories. Arriving at boot camp... The crackle of gunfire at the outdoor shooting range... Immersive classes on how to repair battle-damaged electronic equipment... Shipping out overseas... The endless heat and sand...

Nolan looked over the items laid out before him. Desert camo jacket with "Simmons" name patch on the breast. A respectable collection of service ribbons and badges. Framed photographs of himself and his buddies from the unit. And a small bundle of brochures that he had been given when leaving the Army—information about veteran benefits, mental health resources, and strategies for reacclimating to civilian life.

These glossy leaflets took him even further back, to the moment when he first noticed an Army recruiter's storefront half a lifetime ago. The promises made by those slick promotional posters were a stark contrast to the gritty Newark streets where he had grown up. Cleanliness. Functionality. A chance to excel, see the world, and make an impact.

He had seized on that opportunity and never looked back—until he did. Stationed around the globe at foreign bases, stateside posts in Illinois and Texas, and finally an honorable discharge after twelve years of service. Any number of opportunities awaited this United States military veteran who possessed advanced electronics knowledge.

But he went back home instead. To help fix up the old neighborhood? Or prey upon the weak, by using his skills to turn their petty vices into big business? Nolan knew very well that his mini-empire had not been built by planting trees or organizing charity runs.

He was also reluctant to admit that, had he not agreed to produce a music video for local kid Clyde Jenkins—the one that became a surprise hit last summer—he might never have changed his ways. Kept rationalizing to himself that he gave structure to the neighborhood kids who had no dads by putting them to work. As if sending them off to tag along with the volatile older guys was any kind of example to be setting for them.

None of this was in keeping with the military's code of conduct, where you did the honorable thing when no one else was looking or the odds were against success. But for the past six years, he too had been weak. And too smart for his own good. A cynic masquerading as a businessman, who perhaps chose the straight path only because there were incentives to do so.

Now he was phasing out the unscrupulous aspects of his operation with quiet urgency, while also transitioning into above-board roles such as manager of his own entertainment production facility. Solidifying gains. Guarding his perimeter. Burying evidence. Papering over the predator who had run a consortium of underground businesses from behind a computer screen, while other people put themselves in danger by doing his bidding in dark alleys and abandoned row houses.

He needed to maintain control of the narrative of his life while his sphere of influence grew among the general public. His story was being told and held up as an inspiration, so certain details had to be massaged or omitted when delivering speeches to schools and volunteer organizations. But the people who didn't have his best interests at heart—ambitious journalists, IRS agents—might already be digging for the unvarnished truth about this self-made man from the Newark projects.

The magnitude of his failure of character weighed on Nolan far worse than any exposé that might come out in the press, however. He could stomach the outside world's contempt if his name was dragged through the mud for a week or two. What he really dreaded was looking himself in the mirror each morning.

So much so, that he had even considered leaving town for good recently. There was a white woman who lived in Connecticut he'd met during an October symposium, and they had hit it off right away. But then he started feeling uncomfortable at the oddest moments—and every time his mind wandered back home.

What it boiled down to, he realized, was that he just didn't want to spend his life surrounded by Caucs. Which maybe also explained why he had originally returned to Newark after getting out of the Army.

He reluctantly broke things off with his new lady friend before the Holy Holidays, and then began declining invitations for any future public speaking engagements.

Because Newark was *his* garden to tend. He needed to uplift his neighbors, his friends, and even reach out to enemies or those hurtling toward self-destruction. Until the graffiti was gone and the boarded-up storefronts alive with black-owned businesses, he had no right to give lectures out of town about how things ought to be done.

Nolan placed the collection of keepsakes from his former life back inside the box. He let out a heavy breath, then walked down the hallway to the slim vertical window that was near the elevator.

He looked out onto the cold city as the sun disappeared behind a haze of winter clouds. Knowing in his heart that money and name recognition meant nothing if you sat atop a dung heap.

Nolan Simmons had always been torn between affection and disgust for these streets. Now they would serve as the proving grounds which revealed whether he had truly led a successful life or not.

He was finally ready for the challenge.

9. A TROUBLED CLOWN

"I can't do it anymore. I'm done."

Ryan Richards was pacing in front of his agent Mel Hedren's desk.

"What do you mean by that?" Mel asked. "Done hosting the show? Come on, you can't be serious!"

"But it's true! I'm tapped out."

"*DDM* just got renewed for a third season. Two months ago, you were all bent out of shape thinking it was gonna get canceled in a Dominguez administration. So what gives, Ryan?"

Richards waved his hand dismissively. He said, "Ancient history. I wanna leave. If it turns out to be a career ender, they're welcome to write in the obituary, 'His psyche died from complications due to ambiguity.' "

"Huh?"

"Mel, think back on the early days of the show."

"Yeah, and?"

"Real good times. It was all so clear-cut then. And everyone was excited! We were doing something, ya know? But now…"

"Now, what?" Hedren looked up at him incredulously. "Your ratings are still through the roof! Even *with* all the new, uh, color combinations, hahaha..."

"Eh, it's losing focus. All these changes on the fly, we're just winging it. The show used to stand for something absolute, Mel! People watched it and were inspired. But now it's part Jerry Springer, part car crash, and part *schadenfreude*."

"You've got to be pulling my leg, Ryan. You were out there doing the biggest cartwheels of your career these past few shows. What gives?"

Ryan Richards sighed. "I am a troubled clown."

"So... is this actually more about what's going on with you? Or..."

"I—my career—and the show are joined at the hip. And considering how much it's changed just recently, what else might they expect me to do next month or a year from now? I'm scared."

"I don't know, Ryan. How much further could it possibly veer away?" Mel fished a handkerchief out of his back pocket and dabbed across his shiny bald head.

Ryan leaned in and wailed, "Why not animals next? Or trees?!"

"Holy Christ. He's lost it..."

"Come on, Melly baby. You know I'm right! How many species have we hunted to the brink of extinction? What about all the adorable little calves cut down before their prime to make veal? Or the geese they force-feed so we can eat pâté at fancy parties?"

"And the trees?" Mel asked softly.

"Earth, man! We're killing the whole planet. Whale bellies full of plastic because their home is a toxic soup. Clear-cutting forests left and right to put up more goddamn condos. Need I go on?"

"Apparently you want to. Do you really think the show would go that route? Seems kinda out there. Or has someone been talking?"

"Nah, this is all me. But they're gonna have to ramp up the tension—and the absurdity—so folks keep tuning in. That's why I want out now. I'm not gonna do my whole song and dance while some spoiled brat prattles on about everyone's carbon footprint. What would the punishment be? Who would even go on trial during that episode? Corporate polluters... or people who litter? 'Cause I tell you what, all those folks who got amnesty eight years ago... They sure as hell left a lot of trash in their wake as part of the migrant caravan."

"Okay, Ryan. You're overloading your brain with all these hypotheticals. You really should rest."

"Whatever you say. Yes, tonight I shall rest my world-weary head upon a goose-down pillow. But pray tell, what sins hath mankind committed to acquire *these* dream-inducing feathers?"

Mel paused and gave Ryan a sympathetic look. The strain was evident in the show host's face. He said, "You know they'll never let you walk away, right? Like it or not, you work for the HRA's PR department. They got too good of a thing going to break up the band just yet."

"Dammit... But I *need* to get out before I lose my freakin' mind!"

"I think you're making a mistake. Can I say that? Take a look at the new shows coming up on the spring schedule. You'll see, Reparations is still a hot ticket!"

Mel pawed through some papers on his desk and opened a copy of the *Tinseltown Talker*.

"What do we got here... Boom! *Credit or Debit?* Everyday people bring in their home inventions, then celebrity judges weigh the benefits to humanity. I love it. What else, what else... Couple archaeology programs catering to the indigenous crowd, and next... *Unpack Your Privilege.* Some kind of Sunday morning roundtable, I don't know... Aha! This is the one I really like. *Pardon the Appropriation.* Can you not see it,

Ryan? They're really starting to have fun with it now. And *you* started it all."

Richards brushed aside the compliment with a wave. "And who are the hosts? Let me have that rag… Mm-hmm, yeah. Boom, yourself! Look at all these hacks. Beverly Orleans talking serious politics? Give me a break. Oh, and Justin Chan in the role of MC dealing with a group of A-listers? Doc, get me out of this lunatic asylum. I've already done my time!"

"Just… think it over. You were the trail blazer. That's got to be worth something."

"Bah. This trend is gonna drop like a stone one day —and I don't want to be on stage when it does."

Mel Hedren pursed his lips. "That's the thing, Ryan. You *were* on stage when the Sentinels first attacked. What would it look like if you turned tail just a few months later?"

"Oh Mel, you sly bastard. I think I'm gonna be sick! How long will *that* debacle chain me to *DDM*?"

"Let's not worry about that right this second." Mel pulled open the top drawer of his desk. "The real reason I wanted to meet today was so I could present you with this." He removed an official-looking envelope and handed it to Ryan, who opened it and read aloud slowly.

" 'Dear Mr. Richards… cordially invite… guest of honor… inaugural celebration… evening of…' Holy shit! Mel, you beaut! I'm going to DC!"

"What can I say? You've earned it. And I'm sure the president thinks so too."

"Wow. Eileen Jeffries-Lao and me. The guy who couldn't get a speaking part in the high school play."

"And now the leader of the free world wants to shake your hand in gratitude. Bravo!"

Ryan Richards floated out of his agent's office and headed for the nearest bar. Not to drown his sorrows as planned, but to celebrate.

10. BEST FOOT FORWARD

The house was silent. Tyrell was at school. Dawna had gone out a while ago to have brunch with some friends. And Octavius was… somewhere.

Myra Jenkins stood at the foot of her bed in the upstairs bedroom. Baby Sarah was sleeping peacefully in her crib over in the corner. Myra looked at the dresses laid out on the comforter.

A crinkled purple spaghetti strap with matching blazer. Plain black ending below the knee. Navy and white horizontal stripes with flared hem. All three were so nice. And tomorrow morning, Myra would put her best foot forward when she left Newark wearing one of them and headed into the heart of New York City—to hopefully change her life forever.

Myra sighed and turned away. She had been agonizing over her outfit for an hour. She wished Clyde was here to tell her some jokes, make her laugh the way he always could. Because right now she was feeling so nervous.

Of course her kid brother would take overnight fame

in stride and move out to Los Angeles like it was nothing. He was still young. Didn't have any of the responsibilities or real-life stresses that she did. Juggling two kids, dealing with a mother who offered too much unsolicited advice—and then there was the tense relationship with the man she loved.

But if Clyde was reaching for the stars while strutting around as DJ Clydoscope, Myra's dreams were much more down to earth—even though they sometimes seemed just as improbable. The odds had been stacked up against her long before she awoke from the stupor of her youth to find herself a mother at age sixteen. Nearly seven years later, Myra Jenkins was suddenly on the cusp of her own small breakthrough.

Because while the world was fawning over Clyde and his music, Myra quietly followed through on her own goal of earning a high school GED. She had also completed nearly a dozen interior design projects for a woman who had befriended her down at the HRA vocational school where she worked as a childcare assistant.

And tomorrow, she was scheduled for an in-person interview at the Regnery School of Art in Midtown Manhattan. They had spoken glowingly of her sample portfolio, and the admissions counselor she'd talked to on the phone made it sound like this meet-and-greet would be a mere formality.

Best of all, they appeared willing to extend her a full-tuition scholarship, or something close to it. Myra didn't know if this offer was merit- or need-based. All that mattered was that someone saw she had potential and they wanted her around—wanted to help her grow and make something of herself.

For Myra, this was what she could control. Not pop music trends. Not the choices Octavius made when he was out of the house. Not the people working at the HRA field office, who made her feel stupid just for asking questions.

She didn't always like the way her mother spoke to her, either. Disrespected her boundaries. Cast a judgmental eye toward how Myra lived her life, even though Dawna herself had raised two kids as a single mother.

Myra always hoped she could do better. Be better. But she'd just never known how. A year ago she never would have believed that this reality was out there, let alone so close to home.

As she gazed around the bedroom of this nice condominium which Clyde's success had paid for, Myra admitted to herself how glad she was that she wouldn't have to rely on his money for her art school classes.

Family was one thing. Pride was another. Myra Jenkins had lived her whole life as a nobody in the shadows. Not even considered a disappointment because no one had ever expected anything from her. But now, she was going to walk proudly into the Regnery administration building wearing a beautiful dress—and there was no telling how bright her own star might shine from now on.

11. UNSTOPPABLE SPIRIT

He couldn't believe it was happening.

As he frantically strummed his black Gibson SG guitar, Chris Donohugh watched nearly a hundred people crash and slam into each other as they swirled around the mosh pit in front of the stage. Another three hundred fans stood nodding their heads safely on the periphery.

Chris took a step to his right, leaning toward a microphone as he shouted, "Storm troop… Beverly Hell!"

After several back-and-forth callbacks with the singer, he moved to the edge of the stage and down-picked the first screaming bluesy chord that led into the guitar solo. Hands reached up to him from below and clawed maniacally in playful celebration of his own fingers dancing high up on the fretboard.

Chris eased back and shrugged his whole body in rhythm with the next riff. The drums pounded a mathematical beat that sounded like a factory cranking out industrial-grade machine parts. A warm swirl of satisfaction enveloped him—he was *back* on stage, and playing in front of the largest crowd of his life.

He glanced around. Behind him, drummer Ken was hitting hard and sending beads of sweat flying everywhere. Far to the left, bassist Ian was whipping his yellow-dyed mohawk like a fan.

And center stage gripping the mic was—not Glenn. No, instead longtime friend and scene veteran Miles Dexter had stepped in to sing at this unexpected Raucous Voice reunion. Just one of the five bands gathered tonight in honor of their missing comrade Glenn Murray.

Tonight We Fight: A Benefit Concert for One Political Prisoner's Legal Fund.

That's what the promo posters said. And here on the Boston venue's walls were handmade signs that proclaimed, "Don't Silence *His* Voice!" and "Free Glenn!"

After Raucous Voice finished their set, Glenn's current band Bleeding the Aggregate would take the stage as headliner. Another guy would sing and try to fill Glenn's larger-than-life combat boots during the performance.

The story was that Bleeding the Aggregate had been on a mini-tour when Glenn simply vanished after one of their shows in West Virginia. They'd been forced to cancel the last two dates, and then slowly word spread throughout the punk scene that one of their own was missing.

His family knew nothing. His current and ex-girlfriends hadn't heard from him. As speculation ran wild, from suspicion of suicide to a drunken fall off a bridge, Chris had a better notion of what might have happened to his childhood friend and former bandmate.

And so it was he who had anonymously circulated vague rumors that Glenn could possibly be in trouble with the law. All he'd hoped for was to discover Glenn's whereabouts, but it had quickly taken on a life of its own...

Suddenly other nameless sources came out of the woodwork offering concrete details. Within three weeks of Glenn's initial disappearance, it leaked out that he was being held at the Wallens Ridge supermax prison in Big Stone Gap, Virginia. No formal charges had been filed, no press releases distributed. Nothing. It was as if Glenn Murray had ceased to exist.

So the punk rock scene jumped into action doing what it did best: rallying together with camaraderie and that unstoppable DIY spirit. It had culminated in this concert—raising money, promoting awareness about Glenn's plight, and for Chris, the opportunity to play music live for the first time in nearly a decade.

As he wrenched toxic bar chords out of his beloved Gibson, Chris Donohugh soaked up the overwhelming sensory joy of this moment. There would be time later to think about Glenn sitting alone in a small cell, and hope that word about the concert had gotten to him. To agonize over the possibility that Glenn's interrogators had gotten *to him*—and that he might incriminate his colleagues in the Sentinels of Jubilee. Chris now deeply regretted the few crumbs of HRA data he had given them in a moment of spiteful weakness when he and Kate were at odds.

He stomped his foot and shook off the dark thoughts. A chorus he'd personally written was coming up, and he intended to howl it with such fury that his own raucous voice might travel far and wide, to penetrate those prison walls and let his spiritual brother know he wasn't alone.

Because hundreds of people had come out to support Glenn Murray against government tyranny.

12. BEYOND LOYALTY AND DOUBT

FBI Special Agent Marcus Young was home. Whatever that meant for a man who often spent months embedded among groups that the government was keeping tabs on. He adopted so many fictitious identities that sometimes he even lost track of himself.

Gun runner supplying a motorcycle gang in the mountainous wilds of California. Prospective buyer of several children being trafficked through the Port of Miami. Disgruntled crane operator plotting with others to bomb the mansion of a governor whose policies had put thousands of blue-collar laborers out of work.

And finally, convert to the Church of Modestianity living at the Mall of Absolution in Bloomington, Minnesota. To monitor that start-up cult and its potentially dangerous leader, a man called the Prescient One.

The fallout from these last six months was almost too much to comprehend as he now sat in the silence of his townhouse in Fredericksburg, Virginia.

Before Marcus had completed his reconnaissance mission, the government arrested the Prescient One—aka Scott Cullen—for aiding and abetting the Sentinels of Jubilee. This hacker group had been designated as a domestic terror organization shortly after claiming responsibility for breaking into the HRA's mainframe back in early October.

But by this time Modestianity had already taken hold of Marcus's heart, and on the day of the dramatic raid, he was out doing humanitarian work at an Iowa medical facility owned by the church. The FBI soon tracked him down as well, and persuaded him to join the pursuit of another person of interest—the musician Glenn Murray.

Since then, his allegiances had not simply been tested, but blurred while navigating the high-stakes arena where politics and federal crime overlapped. Playing chess—or a game of chicken—with the bureaucratic state that buttered his bread and told him how high to jump.

Because Marcus had most definitely made compromises with himself. Committed sins of omission during the course of his official duties. Begun to question the depth of his commitment to his newfound faith. And been forced to arrest the man who possessed more integrity than anyone he knew.

Glenn Murray. The rough-edged rock singer with no credentials and seemingly nothing to lose. Who had lost his freedom when events… or his conscience… or the need to provoke a denouement… Whatever his true motivation, Glenn had essentially forced Marcus to arrest him so that—to *protect* Marcus! Because this FBI man was also caught in the drama surrounding America's new reality of living in a restitution-based surveillance state.

After Marcus turned Glenn over for processing, the month of December had passed in a haze. First, the Bureau honored him at a commendation ceremony in which he was showered with praise. Several wild parties followed, and he figured that his bosses were trying to help him ignore any temptations to reconsider his near-defection to Modestianity.

He appreciated their efforts, their understanding, their willingness to forgive his lapse of judgment. Because they knew very well the types of temptation that embedded agents faced. Sex, money, drugs, power. The old identity wavering after months isolated from family and friends.

But now back home with no wife or children of his own to ground him, and only commuting into the local FBI office as needed, Marcus Young felt himself drawn into an uncertain realm. He was beyond loyalty and doubt. Had transcended right and wrong as defined by the hard rules of laws and organizations. He was shell-shocked from time spent in the trenches of a war where no one was shot or killed.

Instead, the weapons were words whose meanings could be twisted for political gain. The mission was not to take land, but confuse and divide populations. And victory was the spiritual demoralization of your foe.

Marcus Young was uneasy about the enfolding nature of this asymmetric conflict. Because he had played a role, or roles, in it. But also because he sensed there would be more ambiguity, more disillusionment —a ship of state slowly sinking down into the bog, perhaps for decades.

All Marcus could do was turn away. He was so fatigued. A stranger in his own home. Blindly probing for answers about what he even wanted out of his own life. After years of sacrifice for career and country, always serving other people—and now waking up at age forty-two to realize that he had neglected to provide himself with anything more concrete to fight for than acronyms and ideals.

But he would not live in such selfless imbalance any longer. Whether that meant throwing in his lot with the Modestians, doubling down with the FBI, or even striking out in a completely new direction—his own interests would have to be a factor from now on.

13. THE REAL YOU

"Of course! I remember that one now. But you was so young!"

"Excuse me?! Just how old do you think I am?"

Clyde Jenkins felt his throat tighten. But that's what happened when you put your foot in your mouth. He tried to recover.

"Nah, I just meant you looked like a kid. But now… you're a woman!" He flashed a smile, and his heart soared when her eyes flickered and she smiled back.

"Awww, ain't you sweet? Come on, let's get some more drinks."

For the next fifteen seconds Clyde felt like he was in heaven. Floating across the room arm in arm with Ayana McGinn, the caramel-skinned former child actress who was now making waves playing more sophisticated roles.

A few moments later, after one of the catering staff had replenished her red wine and his rum-and-cola, they turned and waded through the living room of this mansion high up in the hills of Studio City.

"Anyway," Clyde said as they slipped out onto the quiet balcony, "tell me more about the real you."

Ayana held out her hand, inspected the long blue-peppermint fingernails, then gave a sigh. "The me beneath these acrylics, you mean? I don't know. Guess I'm boring."

"You? No way! All the shows you been in? That's got to be exciting."

"You know, Clyde, my dad used to joke that he wished someone would've gave him a furniture dolly back when I was born. Because that's been my life—always moving back and forth between auditions, acting classes, over to set, on and on. So when I'm not working, yeah, boring is good."

"But you're here tonight, right?"

She chuckled. "You're so green. And it's adorable! But this is a *work* party. You never know who from the industry you might run into."

"Oh," Clyde said, slowly realizing why Eddie had insisted that they attend this stuffy Saturday night affair.

Just then a tall white man with gelled-back hair stepped onto the patio. "Ah, there you are!" he said to Ayana. "Will you be able to… in a few?" He nodded back toward the living room.

"Of course. Just a second. Jerry, this is my new friend Clyde."

The man reached out and shook hands.

Clyde said, "Hi, nice to meet ya."

"Jerry's my agent. Like I said, work party."

"Haha, yes indeed," the man said with a shrug of the shoulders. "So Clyde, what do you do?"

"I sing, and rap. I'm here with Mr. Pryor. Eddie. You might—"

Clyde watched the smile disappear from Jerry's face. The man turned to Ayana and whispered harshly, "Do you not realize who this guy is?"

"DJ… ummm." She blushed, dropping her head

with a smile as she reached out and tickled the top of Clyde's hand. "DJ Cutie."

"Well, there'll be nothing cute happening with your career if you two are seen together in the tabloids. Come on back inside, I've got someone *important* for you to meet."

"Hey now, boss!" Clyde protested. "I ain't done nothing to her, or you. Why you get to interrupt? I know y'all is doin' business, but at least let me get her number first."

Jerry scowled at Clyde, then addressed Ayana again. "This clown is the one who wrote 'Fly So High.' "

"I know," she said. "He told me. I heard it a few times awhile back. So?"

"Uh… Ayana, darling, where do you think the funding for *Kentucky Bless* comes from? The HRA! And you do want your character to return next season, right?"

Clyde saw confusion and then sadness wash over Ayana. Heard her say quietly, "Oh." Watched her turn away from him and reenter the party with Jerry close behind.

He took a sip of his drink, but it didn't taste good now so he dumped it over the railing. As he looked out into the cool night, he heard the sliding door open and then Eddie's loud voice.

"Clyyyde! There's my main man." Eddie hoisted up his beer glass as he approached. "Hey, why so glum? Come rejoin the fun. Somebody I know wants to introduce himself. Oh, and let's get you fixed up with another drink while we're at it."

Clyde stuffed his frustration down and followed Eddie into the house. He would put on a smile and talk to whoever, then try to slip Ayana a piece of paper with his phone number on it before the party ended.

Otherwise, he might need to write a new love song just for her…

14. A LEADER'S JOURNEY

President Jeffries-Lao cycled through the tabs on her computer screen. News articles and videos chronicling the wave of protests around the country that were aimed at her administration. As expected, many Debtors couldn't face the prospect of another four years out of power without throwing a final tantrum before her inauguration.

Then there were the rallies pleading leniency for members of the Sentinels of Jubilee who had been detained. Here Eileen planned to make several gracious concessions in the spirit of moving the nation forward. Implicated Dramacrat Congresshuman Neil Thornton would be freed in exchange for resigning his House seat—which he had in fact won a fourth term to serve, despite being arrested the night before the election.

Also irksome was the benefit concert in Boston which held up some incarcerated musician as a "political prisoner," despite the evidence suggesting that he was an SOJ accomplice. Eileen's advisors had brought this story to her attention because most of the attendees were left-leaning. The takeaway being that just weeks after voting to re-elect her, they were now putting personal loyalties ahead of what benefited the big picture.

Another group of agitators were those kooks up at the Mall of Absolution. Not only were they hosting outrageous masses at home in support of their imprisoned leader, they'd also mobilized the ranks of their satellite churches nationwide. Eileen and her team were deeply disturbed by the passionate spectacle of the so-called Million Modestian March. These dozens of gatherings, which averaged a thousand attendees who were all decked out in asinine teal and silver costumes, proved enough to force her hand.

But only *after* Scott Cullen, aka the Prescient One, had been humbled, humiliated, and spilled his guts. Not just by confessing to his involvement with the Sentinels, but also detailing the inner workings of his brainchild, the Church of Modestianity. And as the cherry on top, Scott made some very disturbing personal revelations while under the influence of tongue-loosening drugs. Oh, what she might do with all that juicy material...

But pragmatism had won out. The Modestians themselves apparently being such true believers, the White House pulse-takers were convinced that the shrewd play was to not make their guru stand trial, let alone force the religion to disband. Because somehow in just a few short years, this color-coded cult had gained a large enough following throughout the United States, that sending in the Feds to scatter them to the wind risked provoking a public relations disaster, if not open conflict.

Better to avoid another potential Waco debacle, and instead return Mr. Cullen to his people a weakened figurehead. Thus neutralized, he would forevermore preach just enough truth to stay in power, but never go so far as to disrupt anyone's agenda.

Eileen now considered the potential benefits of keeping Congresshuman Thornton in place after all. *That* would be one vote she could always count on. He might even be persuaded to take the lead in supporting a series of space initiatives her administration planned to unveil in the fall months...

Jeffries-Lao understood that a leader's journey was long, and often required calling audibles or taking unconventional paths to get across the finish line. Magnanimous gestures made people feel like they were being seen, heard, and catered to. Sometimes all it took was the use of symbols to garner sentimental press coverage as you tossed crumbs to the aggrieved.

And while the masses were out celebrating a trivial victory, your forces moved ahead to fortify real gains. What were a few million dollars donated to some charity but a bargain, when the tectonic shifts facilitated by your laws, executive orders, and bureaucratic outposts were everlasting?

Eileen turned her attention to more positive news. The latest polls showed that her approval among Afrigro-Americans was virtually as high as at the start of her presidency. They still believed in her. That she was their champion and would always fight for them.

She recalled her first attempt to alleviate their plight while serving as California's governor. Appalled by the conditions of black homelessness in cities like Los Angeles and San Francisco, Eileen had spearheaded humane policies to help get drug addicts and the mentally ill out of their filthy tents, as well as bring purpose to the daily lives of those who rode public transit for hours on end. It was one of her most heartfelt political initiatives—which also delivered practical results. Because in clearing a path to restore these poor souls' dignity, she had reopened the sidewalks for business.

And now, nearly a decade later, after having achieved more for Afrigro-Americans than anyone but perhaps Abraham Lincoln, President Eileen Jeffries-Lao had the luxury of taking stock and contemplating her next act in a way that the assassinated emancipator never could.

What crossed her mind was unprintable. Too callous. Too politically *raw* to be spoken outright in a society beholden to politeness. But the truth was that they had all used each other to get here. Had allied to achieve objectives that were certainly noble, but which ultimately had a shelf life.

Soon Eileen would begin the decoupling process, because the world did not begin or end with the needs and pleas of Americans of African descent. They had wanted long-overdue justice and Eileen's administration delivered it—game over.

Were they willing or able to accept that the ledger had finally been settled? That it was time to stand on their own two feet and seize control of their destiny? Not that Eileen had any plans of turning her attention back to the much-maligned Caucmerican crowd...

Because it wasn't even *the world* that beckoned now. Using the HRA to help other former colonial powers patch up their reputations was an important next step, but far from the endgame. Successful space exploration would only be possible if humanity harnessed all of the best minds that globalism had brought together—in technology, science, medicine, and yes, even government.

The universe itself awaited, and Eileen Jeffries-Lao was ready to deliver planet-transcending results during her second term.

15. ULTIMATE PARADOX

"What's up with all these hackers going free after just a slap on the wrist? When *we* get in trouble, they work us through the system hard!"

The man sat down and slapped his leather gloves against his thigh. As the gathered crowd voiced its agreement, a woman wearing a beige dress stood up and said, "We can't just accept that that's the way it is. We got to hit the streets and be heard!"

Loud applause echoed throughout the church meeting hall. Before the woman retook her seat, she added, "And you, Reverend Witherspoon, ought to take the lead."

Matthias Witherspoon eased off the edge of a table up front. He said, "Go out into the streets and do what? Hold up signs—or burn our city down?"

"We gotta let 'em know we feel betrayed after all that big talk before the election," someone hollered. "Supposed to bring the Sentinels to justice!"

Matthias waited patiently as several others vented their frustrations about how the government was disrespecting Afrigro-Americans. He nodded his head after each person said their piece.

Someone pointed a finger at him and demanded, "Well?!"

Reverend Witherspoon pointed back and said, "Well, what? I've been telling you for weeks now that something like this could happen. That it was *bound* to happen. If you had believed me instead of plugging your ears, maybe I *would* help y'all get a street protest going. But now? No way. It's too late."

The lady in beige called out, "What you said, was that the HRA might start pulling away from us. We're all used to broken promises, Reverend." There were murmurs of agreement as she paused. "But letting the people who tried to *end* Reparations walk? No, yourself. That is disgusting! How can we witness such an injustice and sit quiet?"

Matthias said, "Mrs. Lloyd, you're not wrong. It's one more slap in the face after God knows how many others. All I'm trying to do is help everyone look ahead, so we don't get blindsided again. We got to be more prescient moving forward."

"There he go," another woman said in a biting tone. "Talkin' all that Modestian talk."

"Yeah! Why'd he come back again?" a voice boomed.

Matthias forced a smile, then sighed. "I came home because I love you all so much. I want what's best for our community. So now... Do you *really* think there's anything we could say that would make the government folks change their minds? They've thought it all through, and bottom line, they got other plans. Bigger plans that got nothing to do with us! So you can go complain in the streets—*or* we make our own plan now, so we won't have to humiliate ourselves begging Caucs for crumbs no more."

After a loud chaotic moment, a man's voice rang out. "How we gonna do that? You got it all figured out or what?"

"I got some ideas," Witherspoon said. "And that's why we get together after services are over. To discuss these more earthly matters. So let's all cooperate, try to work it out, and find happiness here in this lovely corner of the world."

"Amen!" an old woman cried.

"You got that part right," Mrs. Lloyd added sarcastically. "Because we sure are gonna need a miracle at the end of all this."

"Aw, don't be so salty, Lady Lloyd!" Witherspoon said. "Maybe it's actually a good thing. Truly. You don't want someone else payin' for us *forever*, do you?"

As the grumbling died down and the crowd settled in, he added, "I sure am sick of hearing why we can't do for our own. We got to quit whining… stop lying to ourselves… and just find a way! Because the world is *huge*. While you carry on about how the white man in America done you wrong, people in *other countries* with ugly legacies of their own are making it happen.

"Did you know, that fifty years ago in Cambodia they killed all the people who were educated? Doctors, scientists—hell, if all you did was wear glasses, they might put a hole in your skull. Yep, almost a quarter of their population died in less than four years' time. And look at 'em now! Those Cambodians may not be number one, but at least they're back in the fight. I bet a couple of y'all are wearing some clothes made over there, in fact.

"Not only that, I could spin a globe, pick any other place at random, and I bet something worse happened there than what you got to complain about. Say what? Price of beef went up? Best friend's in jail? Your leg hurts? Ha! Tell that to the people in Syria, who your best friend Barack Hussein bombed all to hell.

"Uh-oh! I done stepped in it now. 'Matthias, you naughty man!' But it's true. Anywhere you look, a hundred years ago or less, people got hit hard by something. Lot of 'em end up moving here to the United States, too. Mm-hmm. Let's chew on that. They never liked us to begin with, these immigrants. Then they see us in action, and back of their mind is saying, 'My uncle got taken away in the middle of the night, and we ain't seen him since. What are these fools complaining about?'

"And you know, they may be right... but dammit, they're also wrong! Why? Because this is *our* country, *our* land! I don't like *no foreigner* sauntering around flappin' his gums about us. No, sir. 'Cause when he steps off the plane, there's a whole system in place to help get him on his way. Free healthcare, nice government housing, school for his kids, family networks too. Anything and everything to give him that soft landing we never got after the boat ride.

"I mean... I *guess* Reparations was supposed to be that. But even if the dollar amount was just right, I say it came way too late. We tired, we broken! We been confused for so long, we don't know what to believe. So we lash out, hit anyone we can—while of course saving the worst for our own kind. Because in our hearts, ladies and gentlemen, many of us hate ourselves.

"Easy as it would be to cook up a fresh batch of poison, what if we took this pledge instead? For one year, we will make the right decisions. We will take the *least*-destructive path. 'Cause let's face it, lot of temptation come a person's way in twelve months, hehe. Can't hurt to try our best, am I right?

"Choose to defuse an argument before it turns to the gun. Pick up those dusty old dumbbells and walk around the block. And when you pass the liquor store, and sneaky Mrs. Kim smiles with those shelves full of booze, you tell her, 'No! I ain't drinkin' none of that tonight!'

"Give me a year, folks. Check in with *each other* every week. One thousand small steps in the right direction, and this congregation will emanate a glow that's sure to spread over to the next town, on and on. Simple as that. Each person doing a tiny bit each day is how you make progress, my people.

"Not by filming yourself yelling, 'I am the greatest!' But ain't that the ultimate paradox? One minute we're down on ourselves, then the next we braggin'. Not about accomplishments, mind you, but sayin' stuff like, 'I'm a king.' 'I'm a queen.' 'We *all* kings and queens.' And then there's my personal favorite, 'Black people is *powerful!*'

"Look, I get it. Some misguided fool put that idea into your head, trying to instill pride or self-esteem or whatever. But my goodness, replacing depression with delusion is *not* the solution! Same reason just 'cause I drop a nice rhyme now and again, it don't make me a world-famous rapper, right? No, ma'am. Matthias is only master of the Sunday morning ceremony, not out at the club on Saturday night…"

The crowd laughed. Reverend Witherspoon took a sip of water, then continued.

"I bet some of y'all caught on to the fact that old Matthias is a student of history. Would you believe me, if I said I found out who the first ever debt protester was? It's true. Somebody who really didn't want their own inconvenient archives seeing the light of day.

"Let's go back a bit. The year is 1982. Yes, that's correct. Long before Baby MARVIN was born and started cryin' and poopin' all over our lives, there was a treasure hunter who went looking for gold in sunken ships all over the world. This gentleman was exploring some wreckage off the coast of Brazil—a country, by the way, which received *four million* of your African cousins. That being forty percent of the total number of slaves shipped across the Atlantic Ocean, for your information. But y'all don't know, y'all don't care, right? Right! Moving on.

"Anyway, the dude dives down and starts poking around this underwater boat. What does he find? Not much in the way of coinage, but there's lots of artifacts. Beautiful vases, pottery... nice stuff for museums. So what was the problem? I'll tell ya what. Those items dated back to Roman times! Fifteen hundred years before the Portuguese first landed on those same shores!

"So did Brazil say, 'Oh my gosh, thank you kind sir for making this incredible discovery. Humanity will be so much richer for the knowledge which you risked your life to acquire'? Heck no! First, they took this adventurer to court to keep him away from the site. Then one day, the Navy went out there and dumped a whole lotta dirt on top of the ship, so no one could get at it anymore. I kid you not!

"And all for what? Money? Prestige? Nope. Brazilian government just didn't want to deal with the hassle, the *inconvenience* of having to rewrite their history books—or their treaties with the mother country, Portugal.

"So look, the next time your local paper prints an article about some dastardly Cauc who got caught burning an old contract he found up in his attic, maybe you'll remember that Matthias said to cut him some slack. We are all weak-willed sinners. And now you know, he ain't the first or the worst offender.

"Let us praise the Lord, because I do love you all. If we remember to stick together, we'll surely make our way through."

16. ANONYMOUS TIP

Work had become a breeze. No more arguing or haggling with the Debtors and Beneficiaries who showed up at HRA branches. Instead, all reasonable claims were processed with a smile, from requests to increase one's monthly stipend to accepting documents that might reduce a person's Debit Score.

Kate Donohugh *had* noticed that the staff was smaller than before the Holy Holidays and New Year's long weekend, but there was always turnover around this time. She simply couldn't believe that all of the missing faces had been let go—or caught in the Sentinels dragnet. Her supervisor Jan remained mum on the subject as well, so Kate just kept her head down and focused on her own job. She herself had already taken two leaves of absence from her Newark office in the past year—and with possibly a third to come, she figured it would be wise not to rock the boat.

The streamlined workflow meant that her department was freed up to tackle new initiatives. Today she was sitting in on a presentation entitled,

"Second Act: The HRA Reaches Maturity." A bubbly male-and-female duo was riffing on all of the upcoming changes

"…after reaching many wonderful milestones. Battles won—"

"—and lost—"

"Now, now, Erica. That's just life!" The man gave a goofy smile. "Which is why it's so crucial to not just have a team—"

"—but the whole organization behind you," the woman said with a declarative nod. "While you all were kicking your feet back and enjoying holiday cheer, the HRA busy bees were finalizing an exciting game plan for 2029…"

"…and beyond!"

The static image of the HRA's green and white logo being projected onto the wall now gave way to a montage of data graphics and stock photos featuring people of all ages and races enjoying each other's company.

"Caring!" the woman shouted. She pumped her fist triumphantly.

"Let everyone know how much you care about them," the man implored.

"Outreach!"

"Don't hide away in that cubicle, friend. The HRA wants to see you in *action!* Mm-hmm."

"Security!"

The man brought a hand to his forehead and simulated peering into the distance. "That's right. If you suspect any fishy business, don't just look the other way. You can submit—"

"—an anonymous tip—"

"—and help save the day!"

The duo did a synchronized celebratory dance

before moving on to the next topic.

Kate looked at her watch and sighed. This meeting would run for another half hour, then she was scheduled for a sit-down with several supervisors and managers that would last two hours. After that, she needed to write the first draft of an article for the department's internal newsletter...

She held her phone below the table surface and typed, "When does the outreach part actually begin?"

Her coworker friend TJ giggled from his seat nearby a moment later, then a reply message came back saying, "More like, out of touch!"

"How much do you think these two get paid for doing this?"

"You mean it isn't *punishment?*"

Kate laughed quietly through her nose as she typed, "Maybe they were on *DDM TV* too."

"Speaking of which... are you off the hook or what?"

"Speak no evil, hear no evil. So, just holding my breath and waiting."

"But, missy... you *did* evil. Scofflaw!"

Kate looked over at TJ and shook her head. He smirked.

"Who's the Southern gentleman again?" she wrote.

"My conscience is clear. Most of us Rowes were too poor to own property, let alone *people*."

"Jerk!"

"Cyberbully."

"Redhead."

At this, TJ snorted before quickly covering his mouth. Kate closed her eyes and held her breath to keep from laughing out loud and making a scene.

Meanwhile the presentation up front continued unabated, as bold statements and animated gestures rammed home each talking point with the power of a slam dunk.

17. EYES INSIDE THE GATES

The paperwork he was required to sign seemed endless. Declarations that he wouldn't speak negatively of the government. Bank drafts transferring portions of his assets to the United States Treasury. Detailed confessions that were most likely transcribed from his drugged-out ramblings.

Scott Cullen wondered why he agreed to such a deal. To cooperate with Eileen Jeffries-Lao's administration and gain release without a trial, so long as he obeyed the provisions of the documents stacked in front of him.

Maybe he believed that the Reparations-as-surveillance-state awakening was inevitable, and that he would rather be a free man during that chaotic time. Or maybe he did it for the Church of Modestianity. To fulfill his prophecy after leaving the Mall of Absolution in chains.

Or the torture had actually broken him. Had completely stripped away his ego and accomplishments and soul, leaving only a liquefied psyche in its wake. If the Prescient One ceased to exist and Scott Cullen was also a shattered slate, then perhaps he would have to create himself out of whole cloth once again.

But he would not do it alone this time. He knew in his heart that something beyond himself had been his guide out of the darkness. It was an element both beautiful and pure, extending the promise of unknown future joys if he dared to survive. And so he had.

This transfixing light had also left the seed of a riddle inside his mind. It whispered, "For a human life to achieve true meaning, one must not simply transcend the process of reacting—but also go beyond the self. To perform acts that emanate *out* as well as build *up*."

But having already lost so much, Scott could not help but wonder if these epiphanies were impossibly grand delusions…

After the documents were signed, he was returned to his cell to collect the personal effects he had accumulated during nearly two months in captivity. These items included the holy books of several esoteric religions from centuries past, a bar of soap which he had whittled into a capital *M*, and a small bag of toiletries.

Scott hoped that the electric blue outfit and cape he had been wearing at the time of his abduction would be returned to him. But one of the guards just laughed and said, "Nope. Government's keeping that stuff as a scalp."

"No great loss," Scott said. "I have others. Casual clothing will suffice."

"Sorry, fella. No can do. That beautiful orange onesie you've got on looks just fine."

"But why? I don't understand. I'll be a free man."

"Oh, you'll see…"

And a short while later, Scott did see. His arrest and

incarceration may have begun in secret, but it all ended with a media circus. He was forced to walk out in the open for nearly three hundred yards, going from the facility's entrance to a transport vehicle which seemed to have been intentionally parked as far away as possible.

So that the frail and haggard Scott Cullen would be exposed to the harsh winter elements, his bright jumpsuit flapping in the swirling winds as he trudged forward. Exposed to the unforgiving cameras of the hundred-strong press corps, which had been invited to maximize his humiliation in the eyes of the world—and his church.

Scott clenched his jaw and endured this shameful walk while flanked by three imposing guards. Were these men in place to keep the reporters from charging, or to dissuade a hidden sniper from attempting assassination on this gusty day?

A youngish business type wearing a sport coat was waiting in the back seat of the van. As Scott took his place across from him, the man said, "Mr. Cullen! Agent Vance. I'll be your escort, as well as two other support vehicles. Got to keep you safe, right?"

"But of course. I'm still a wealthy man, despite the close shave your employers just gave me."

"Hey, do the crime, pay the dime. But I might suggest you spend some of that leftover cash at an all-you-can-eat buffet. 'Cause you look like absolute shit."

"That's what happens when you're fed a steady diet of brain-relaxing chemicals." Scott pointed at his stomach. "The weight, here and on one's conscience, falls right off."

"Oh, so you really have lightened your burden? I swear, you and those effing Sentinels… Made us look like idiots."

Cullen noticed that Vance was absently tapping at the side of his blazer. He said, "Is this really an escort… or are we en route to some sort of Mafia killing, complete with a ready-made patsy?"

The agent laughed. "I wish. But no, Your Prescience. Just a not-so-subtle reminder that we'll be watching you closely from here on out. Break the terms and we'll break—"

"Nothing," Scott interrupted. "Which is why I'm getting out now. Short of murder, there's nothing more you or anyone else can do to hurt me."

"Heh, I guess we'll see about that. Just keep your nose clean, Scottie. We've got eyes inside the gates."

"Spies at the Mall, you mean?"

"All of them fervent believers. They love you, and they love Mod too. Oh, yeah…"

The ride to the airport proceeded in silence. Scott Cullen remained calm, knowing that very soon he would begin the next major project to redefine his life.

18. PARALLEL DIRECTIVE

"Uh-ohhh…"

Nolan Simmons clenched his front teeth together and glanced uncomfortably around the room. He reread the tabloid headline on his computer screen.

Pre-Columbian Dirt Muddying Reparations Waters!

Quickly he scanned the article for prominent names. So far, all of the politicians and celebrities mentioned were C-list at best.

"But for how long?" he said to himself, grabbing a tablet as he rose from the leather swivel chair and exited the business office. He rode the elevator down one floor and flashed a key card outside a room that was dark except for the glow of nearly a dozen computer screens. He cleared his throat after entering. The boys inside slowly turned away from their workstations.

"Now listen up," Nolan said sharply, then held the tablet aloft. "I just sent this news story to y'all. And if it is to be believed, then our friend MARVIN is working on a parallel directive."

"What's that mean?" a kid wearing glasses asked.

Another boy stood up. He moved his arms jerkily and said in a robotic voice, "Macro… Aggregating… Restitution… Vector… Input… Navigator."

Everyone burst out laughing.

Nolan waited a moment before addressing the first boy's question. "Zeke just said 'what's that mean?' Don't none of y'all nerds see what's going on?" After getting no response, he added, "It means the Sentinels ain't actually dead!"

This claim prompted some nods and murmurs from the young computer whizzes. Their jobs centered around promoting local creative projects that Nolan was supporting, but ever since the Sentinels of Jubilee struck back in early October, they had also been keeping tabs on all things HRA-hack-related.

"So, Mister S.," another boy began, "how do we fit in with all of that?"

"Excellent question, Omar. Now, if y'all don't mind while I just—" Nolan nudged the light dimmer up a step, so that he wouldn't crash into anything while delivering his pitch. "Look, the normies might not see it yet, but articles like this, even if they start out in the gossip papers… It means the writing is on the wall, y'all."

"For who?" was the boys' reply.

Nolan chuckled. "Not who, but when. Two reasons. First, it's admitting they might change how far back the MARVIN tech goes digging. And second, could be the Sentinels are basically saying, 'We can't stop Reparations from spreading, so eff it, let's go for broke!' And by doing it that way—by accelerating the process—they might blow up the HRA's timetable for rolling out in other countries. Y'all feel me now?"

After seeing a few tentative shakes of the head,

Nolan shouted playfully, "What?! You're supposed to be geniuses, that's why I hired you! Alright, alright, I know you're only *technicians*. Look, the government planned to do everything on a certain schedule—to maximize the money getting paid out while maintaining social stability. Y'all know they hit that speed bump couple months back, then got themselves fixed up. But! This right here looks like it could be a damn iceberg!"

"C'mon, Nolan," Zeke said. "Help us *see*. What we supposed to do?"

"Y'all are gonna help MARVIN out."

"What?!"

"That's right. Don't matter if you don't understand why, but Reparations as we know it is done, son! Cooked goose. Soon as a few top-bill celebs or all-star point guards start getting lit up by their *unauthorized* Debit Scores, oh my God, will we be in for a show! Afrigros gonna be *beggin'* Jeffries-Lao to shut it down once and for all."

Several of the boys stood up as Nolan doubled over in a fit of laughter.

"So what y'all are gonna do," he continued, "is help find more data that's older than 1492. And hell, anything you can get out of Africa, India, Aztecville, wherever, grab it all."

"Yeah, yeah!" the boys cheered.

"Each of you will get a budget of a hundred bucks a day. Post classified ads, information requests, whatever you think might get the documents flowing into our network. Gonna be a lot of international work too, so use your translation software, generate regionally sensitive avatars with the portrait blender... and have fun! In one week we'll analyze the early results, tweak our methods, then increase funds as necessary. How you geeks feel now?"

"In MARVIN we trust!" Omar declared as he thumped a fist against his chest. All the other boys laughed.

"Damn right! Glad you remembered that line."

"You only played the track a hundred times," someone muttered sarcastically. "How could we forget?"

Nolan whipped his head around and peered through the darkened room. "Who said that? Come on, don't be afraid."

A hand went up slowly.

"Alright, Mr. Philpot. Very funny. Just be sure when you say your prayers before bed tonight, remember to thank God for DJ Clydoscope. 'Cause without him, you'd all be playing dice out on your front stoops. And dead broke too!"

As Nolan walked back toward the elevator with a jump in his step, he wondered how Clyde was adapting to life in Los Angeles. Because the wolves out there were willing to take advantage of *anybody*, regardless of gender, age, or skin color.

A city of equal opportunity predators, all selling that dream...

19. BETWEEN TWO WORLDS

Luis Ortega felt awake for the first time in his life.

He realized that he had always been a passenger on someone else's journey. An accessory to their story, their agenda. First as a baby, when taken from Mexico by his parents to cross into the United States illegally. And then more recently, appearing on that Reparations-themed TV show to be used as a prop for whatever those people were trying to achieve.

Luis now sensed that beneath the desire to honor his family, who had risked so much for a chance at a better life, he was also subconsciously driven to prove himself worthy of being in America. The country that had agreed to adopt him and millions of other foreign-born people, despite the fact that they hadn't stood in line. And yet... there was some mysterious touch of fear within it all.

An apprehension that would not take solid form. Because everything about his life seemed vague. Nothing was definite or reliable. His entire conscious existence had taken place in the United States, but every day someone reminded him that he was Mexican, a Latizo, a Minorican...

Perhaps his escape from the *DDM TV Live* stage was the first in a series of desperate attempts to... latch onto something *other* than imposed identity. To declare that he, Luis Ortega, was his own person. But, if the main reason for pursuing an associate's degree was in order to become the first college graduate in his family, then even that accomplishment might not be enough to sustain him.

Especially now, when it was a diverse group of Minoricans—and not resentful white supremacists— who had gotten in his face with *threats* saying he should go back to the correct ethnic pen. Meanwhile his Cauc professor at LACC, Mr. Smiley, he wanted everyone to succeed...

These conflicting thoughts were too much for the normally easygoing Luis. He felt paralyzed, and wondered if he really *was* trapped in some sort of cage. Because if achieving educational goals could not liberate or define him, what else did he have? How would he even go about creating a new version of himself?

Luis thought about his girlfriend Cristina who lived in Boulder, Colorado. She made him feel really good when they were together, but now he was even having doubts about why she liked him. They had only met because two months ago, a group of young people who were protesting the Direct Descendant Match program hoped to use his notoriety to gain traction for their anti-HRA lawsuit.

They were already holding him up as a near-mythical figure by the time Cristina, who was of mixed Latiz-Caucmerican ancestry, contacted them in hopes of deferring her own DDM call-up on the Debtor side.

Luis had instinctively shied away when they appeared at his parents' house unannounced, but the tragic look in Cristina's eyes as she pleaded for help out on the driveway… He simply couldn't resist trying to live up to the vaunted reputation of the "Saint Luis" who was praised in the group's hymns.

But the tides were shifting aggressively now. Luis knew that he couldn't be so passive anymore and survive. He would have to push forward—or lash out—to avoid being completely crushed.

He tried to think of anyone who could give him the proper guidance as he took the first bold steps in his nineteen years of life. His parents and other older relatives couldn't help. Mentally, they acted as if they were still back in Mexico. They didn't understand anything about his experience as the boy who straddled the fence between two worlds.

Cristina was sweet, and he hoped they could be together, but she was always so busy with her college gymnastics team. If he was lucky enough to rely on her heart, it was probably too much to think that she could help resolve his identity crisis.

Suddenly Luis perked up and smiled. He *did* know one person who would definitely offer some unique advice.

He opened the contacts app on his phone and brought up the entry for Ryan Richards. He typed, "hey ryan its luis… remember me??"

Five minutes later, he heard the phone ring.

"What's up, kiddo!" The man's voice was as loud and boisterous as ever.

Luis said, "Hey, Mister Ryan. Thanks for calling me back. I hope I—"

"Of course, bud! I wish half the guests on my show were as cool as you. So what's going on out in LA, bro?"

"Actually, I hit you up because things are kinda weird. I need like, some help."

"Okay, uh… sure. What's got you out of whack?"

Luis took a long breath. "Man, you're so natural, so smooth. I just… sometimes I feel really out of place. Like invisible one minute, and then they're telling me what to do."

"Ahhh…" Ryan said with a sympathetic chuckle. "What you're talking about is *respect*. You want people to know you're more than a chair they can just move around."

"Hmm. Sometimes I'm kinda watching everything happen, you know? I *wanna* speak, but like, maybe I'm not really there?"

"Well, *I* hear you, amigo. Loud and clear. And hell, I really appreciate you reaching out to me. 'Cause Luis, I'm a real person, too. The truth is, I *became* the Ryan Richards that people know and love—or loathe. So take it from this old loudmouth here, sometimes ya just gotta put your foot down and shout, 'I'm me, goddammit!' Let the world know you are somebody, that you're *good*, and it really ought to consult you from time to time *before* making all the decisions."

"Yeah!" Luis was starting to feel electrified. "Because, you know, I do everything I'm supposed to. But then… people come up, they get on me anyway."

"Who? Are you talking about the HRA, or… not me, I hope?!"

"Oh, no, not you! It's these guys at school. Buncha Latizos, Afrigros… They got in my face 'cause I didn't wanna do the DDM stuff."

Ryan sputtered his lips. "Christ… Effin' bullies, man! What can ya do? What can *we* do? I say fight fire with fire. Why not use all the surveillance to your advantage? I assume they threatened you in public, so you should pay a visit to the school's IT department and have 'em pull that footage."

"Aw, no… I can't do that. If I get them in trouble, maybe they'll tell one of their friends to cut me up."

"What the… ? Okay, in that case, what are your other options? Run, hide, drop out of school? It's no good, Luis. You *have* to stand up for yourself. This is one of the most important moments in your life."

"Really?!" Luis smacked his forehead. "I already had like two of them this year!"

"Ha! You are a funny one, Mr. Ortega. Look, I gotta head out soon for some work crap. But just remember, *you* are the man who stuck a middle finger in the HRA's face. You did it first, before anyone else had the guts. So I really think that in the moment, you'll find there's more courage in that heart of yours than you realize."

Luis smiled slightly. "Thanks, Ryan. You're awesome. So… how's everything going with you?"

"Ah, you know. I'm a puppet with great perks. But soldier on we must, fine sir!"

"Cool, cool. But seriously, thanks again. You're a good friend."

"Shucks, kid. You just made my day. Chin up out there…"

20. PRISONER EXCHANGE

The president's busy schedule of pre-inaugural events next took her to Forrest City, Arkansas. Here on this bright but brisk Wednesday morning, a crowd of several hundred was gathered outside the front entrance of a stout official building made of gray stone.

Eileen stood on a low riser with several dozen other people. As a crush of cameras jostled for position up front, a white woman with tousled gray hair approached the podium. She adjusted her horn-rimmed glasses, then began.

"Oh my, what a wonderful turnout. For those who don't know, my name is Marjorie Dorfman. I am a professor of political science at the University of Michigan, Ann Arbor. And we're here today because of a question that I posed during a lecture two years ago. I asked, 'How can a privileged college student majoring in criminal justice turn their passion from theory into actual real-world experience?' Well, the movement that sprouted from that idea has most certainly redefined the concept of a summer internship, I should think."

This last line was met with laughter and then rousing applause.

"And so," Dorfman continued, "today we mark the conclusion of our prisoner exchange program's maiden six-month voyage. New volunteers will be checking in, while those who have completed their terms hand off the proverbial baton. Now, shall we?"

A dozen fresh-faced male Caucmericans wearing street clothes came forward and flanked the professor on her left. They smiled and gave a wave to the assembled newspeople. Then, from behind, a door swung open and out came an equal number of casually dressed Minoricans. They stepped onto the riser and fell into position on Dorfman's other side.

"The gentlemen to my right have all served lengthy sentences behind these walls. But with years of model behavior to their credit, and all soon eligible for parole, they were ideal candidates for our new pilot program." Dorfman glanced over her shoulder and smiled. "Sirs, welcome back to the world!"

The men raised their arms in triumph as the crowd cheered. A few moments later Dorfman added, "Now, tag your partners in!" The young Caucs raced past the parolees, slapping hands loudly as they hopped off the stage and ran through the prison's front entrance.

Once the commotion had died down, Professor Dorfman said, "We also happen to have a *very* special guest here with us today, so I won't keep you waiting much longer. But since the reinforcements have just gone inside, I say out with the old and in with the new!"

The prison door opened once again. Now a third group emerged. Ten young Caucs in orange jumpsuits staggered out into the light. Several were emaciated, and their faces ashen. One man's arm was bandaged in a heavy cast. Another limped noticeably and struggled up the riser's few steps. The man with a teardrop tattooed beside his right eye flashed a smile, and it was apparent that several of his upper teeth were missing.

The crowd gasped. Eileen Jeffries-Lao, who had remained silent and inconspicuous until this moment, was horrified. She leaned toward the staffer at her side and hissed, "You need to get me out of here!" The other woman stared back at her like a deer caught in the headlights.

"My, my," Professor Dorfman beamed. "Here they are! Our brave first wave of participants, who now have intimate knowledge of what life is like on the inside for the people we represent as advocates. Let's hear it for these future revolutionaries in the field of criminal justice reform!"

The applause was more subdued now. The crowd murmured in quiet, anxious tones. Dorfman continued to clap loudly even after everyone else had gone silent. She sighed.

"Such a proud moment for us all. But the best is yet to come. It is my privilege and honor to introduce to you our great leader, the President Re-Elect, Mrs. Eileen Jeffries-Lao!"

Everyone clamored loudly as Eileen emerged from the rear of the stage. She radiated in a yellow-gold skirt suit, and her hair had been done up with bulbous volume. She grasped Dorfman's hand warmly, and held the grip with her free hand when she felt that the other woman intended to move in for a hug.

Speaking into the microphone, she said, "Thank you, Professor Dorfman. And kudos for your... truly unique vision. I'm sure we all have high hopes for these fine gentlemen beside us, who have no doubt earned the right to re-enter society ahead of schedule."

Eileen nodded graciously at the cluster of parolees,

who were now positioned much further back on the riser and flanked by four members of her Secret Service detail.

"Perhaps my appearance here today will be considered somewhat ironic, but I have an important announcement to make. One that I believe will, in its own way, demonstrate my administration's efforts to think long term. Not only toward increased understanding, but also with reconciliation in mind. Last night, I signed Executive Order number 14215. It authorizes the closure of all HRA-affiliated debtors' prisons within six months. Each inmate's obligation shall be marked as paid in full, and their records wiped clean."

The audience gasped in shock once again.

"Now, now everyone. Please hear me out. We've all come so far these last few years. And while the events of recent months have been challenging, we must see them as opportunities to grow. My priority has always been to steer our country safely ahead. So believe me when I say, we won't make it if we see fellow citizens who disagree with us as potential lifelong enemies. We've simply got to find a way to put the animosity behind us. And I assure you it will be worth it, because there is so much more coming for us all to look forward to…"

Eileen continued speaking for several minutes, but sensed that her words were falling on deaf ears. When she concluded her remarks, the crowd gave its most lackluster response of all.

She eased away from the podium and closed her eyes while Professor Dorfman offered some final thoughts. She deeply regretted the scheduling blunder which had put her in this awkward position. It would have been wiser to announce her olive branch of an executive order from the controlled environment of the White House.

21. BE MY ROCK

Octavius Blount wrapped his large hands over the top of a chairback and leaned his weight forward. He said, "So you're gonna be spending a bunch of time up at that school, then?"

"You're supposed to say, 'Congratulations, Myra.' "

"Oh… yeah. 'Course. You know I want the best for you. I'm just tryin' to see how it's all gonna play out."

Myra left the kitchen and walked past Octavius into the dining area. "You mean like, how we goin' to fix our schedules so the kids get to where they need to be?"

"Something like that, yeah I guess." Octavius began to pace. "But…"

"There's something more, isn't there? It's bothering you, too."

"I mean… Look, Clyde got out. Now you goin' legit. And I know what your moms thinks of me, even if she talk nice to my face."

"But baby, she *loves* you! She always stands up for you."

"*Stands up?* What about me needs standing up?"

"I don't know! But maybe, it sounds like, you were about to lay it all out?"

Octavius shook his head. "God damn, I got some kinda pressure on me in this house. Myra... You the mother of our little princess. And now you're heading up into that *other* world, with white folks and all they different rules—"

"Oh, so you don't think I can run with them? That I can't do the work? Thanks!"

"No, girl! I'm sayin' you *can*. And me, the way I make my money... I don't think none of them school folks'll want to see me—or more like, pretty soon *you* won't want any of them to know about me."

Myra brought a hand up to her cheek. "Octavius, I can't believe you're doing this to me. I didn't think that anyone could spoil my moment, but now you're making me feel sick."

"Ha, how you think I feel? I'm the one who sees a future where I get kicked to the curb, and you end up this big interior design lady or whatever."

"You really think I'm already planning all that out? I don't even have any textbooks yet!"

"I ain't sayin' you doin' anything wrong. No blame goin' out to anyone here. But I sure as hell see the writing on the wall. And maybe normally, the old me, he would just jump in the car and be gone. Long gone! But for real, I am *trying* to be on it witchu. So that's it. That's what I got to say."

Myra leaned into his tall frame and wrapped her arms around him. "Octo-Man, you know that I adore you. I see you every time I look at Sarah's eyes. Just... let's take it one day, one week as it come. 'Cause you know, if you maybe a little bit scared, I might be too! I'm the one who got to go up there and pretend I belong.

I don't know how to act at a school like that. So come on, be my rock, please."

Octavius relaxed and eased away. He said, "Okay, I see what's up. We both got our worries. Guess only time will tell."

"Exactly. But I'm glad it's you I got on my team. The man who got my back."

"I got yo' back, no doubt. Got yo' booty too! Now come on in and give me a kiss."

Myra smiled. "Yeah. That's my Mista Blount. I give you a kiss alright."

22. LEGAL KNOTS

"Ah, Marcus!" Sabine Plotz rose from her chair behind the oak desk and opened her arms for a hug. "What brings you into the belly of the beast?"

FBI Special Agent Marcus Young embraced his old law school friend and said, "All hands on deck. They want this inauguration to go off without a hitch."

"I'm sure. Have there been any… credible threats?"

"I'd say it's more the volume of the chatter. A few crackpots with too much time on their hands are probably responsible for most of it."

"Well," Plotz said while retaking her seat, "I'm glad you had some free time to stop by for a visit."

Marcus sat down in one of the two guest chairs. "When I heard you'd taken an office in DC, how could I not?"

"*Temporary* office," Sabine said with a smile. "Our little lawsuit seems to have won the we've-got-their-attention lottery."

"Oh? Lay it on me."

"Marcus, since you've been out running around in

the field for so long, you might have forgotten what a grind this can all be. The pursuit, the preparation, then blindly throwing darts at the wall hoping something will stick."

"I remember… enough," he said with a chuckle. "It's why I had to get the hell out of the office for good."

"Right. Well, I was involved with several other HRA-related cases before this one fell into our laps back at the firm in So Cal. And let me tell you, all of those were a frustrating slog at best. I mean, the administration would never post *this* on their rah-rah page, but a hell of a lot of government lawyers have *also* benefited from the HRA jobs program these last few years. If you catch my drift. And with good reason, too, because their track record is no joke."

"But your new case is different?"

Sabine looked down and fiddled with a pen. "It is, but I don't want to get too cocky. Especially because much of the power behind our case comes not from my legal skills, but *who* my clients are."

"Bennies."

"Exactly. Although, not all of them. Some are, for lack of a better word, white allies. And others still are mixed-race, and all of the complexities that go along with that."

"Ah."

"But the unifying theme is that they're all *young*."

"Which means what?"

Plotz paused. "Think about how different our country looks today compared to just twenty years ago, when you and I were around college age. Even if everything wasn't great back then, there was more *certainty*. A lot of truths you could still rely on. But today that narrative authority has been lost. Now imagine if you'd been born in 2008. A lifetime of economic struggles, lingering wars, political chaos… Who could you trust growing up in that reality? I think that this upcoming generation has forged a unique alliance—both online and in person—that on the surface *looks* diverse, but the glue is that they all share a common lived experience."

"Let me think about this," Marcus said. "They've been grappling with the consequences—or fallout—of the policies that previous generations put in place. And now that they're technically adults, they're making their own choices."

"Very good, Special Agent. *Everything* has aftereffects that are both unpredictable and uncontrollable."

"Mm. So, what's next for the case?"

"This!" Sabine thumped her fist down onto a tall stack of folders and binders. "It's the substance of the case, formally speaking. As you can see, a lot for everyone to get through, even if they run keyword filters through their digital files. Regardless, I think we've got a good shot to win round one—but who can ever predict what the result might be at the appellate level? Still, moving through each stage eats up more time. And all the while, this ragtag coalition of plaintiffs will be out there celebrating their initial victory in the streets and online. As I've heard them say many times, imagine what would be possible for their peer group if the government would just get off their backs."

"Wow!" Marcus rubbed his hands together excitedly. "That's some kind of an escalation. And it sounds like they're making a statement that transcends this one particular program."

"Indeed. They want *everyone* out of their lives. Call

them libertarians, no-one-is-illegal-istas, whatever. The point is they are a new breed, a new kind of army, and there's no silencing them."

"They've got the perfect cover, too. What's the point of the HRA, if Beneficiaries can't speak for themselves?"

"I know," Plotz said, leaning back and exhaling breezily. "Sometimes I feel like I'm working this case on cruise control. I'm not saying I can't lose, but in no way will the government win—in the abstract sense, at least."

Marcus gave a little grumble. "Something about this makes me nervous, though. Just now you called them a new breed. You know, a long time ago I used to think about how *I* was something new, or unique. Being mixed-race was still fairly uncommon when we grew up, and nothing like what we see everywhere today. I could have even been called a 'minority among minorities,' because I didn't speak or act in a way that certain people would call 'black'. But you know, I still had *American things* to fall back on. Like baseball culture. That gave me a life. A lifestyle."

"I remember you showing me a few clips of you hitting home runs, way back when."

"Yeah, good times. I haven't even played catch in years… But anyway, this young crew. Growing up in an era of uncertainty. Loss of faith in every sector, where even your gender might be a toss-up. Amnesty for lawbreakers one year, then punishment for your ancestors' crimes the next. Where's the stability or consistency? No wonder their loyalty lies not with race or nationality, but with those other kids who also got tossed into the melting pot at public school."

"But now," Sabine said, "that dish isn't turning out like the chef wanted. And so…"

"You think there's more to come?"

"Maybe she'd rather dump it out than close the whole restaurant down."

"How… how would she do that?"

"The chef's got four years left on her lease, right? So you get out there this weekend and do your job. Keep the president safe so we can find out."

Marcus smiled. "But you'll be ready, Sabi, won't you?"

"Let's just say, as much as I wish I was back in California instead of freezing my butt off in DC, this office might not be so temporary after all."

"So, the HRA's even providing *you* with job security. Yup, the lady is getting paid…"

"Don't give me any of *that* lip. My family's from Germany."

23. A DIFFERENT KIND OF DARKNESS

Clyde Jenkins was in a funk. Something about this LA experience didn't feel right. As he eased into a chair out on the balcony of this condo which Eddie Pryor had set him up in temporarily, he thought about his encounter with Ayana McGinn.

He had in fact been able to hand her his phone number when her agent Jerry was facing away talking to someone else. But now, it was days later and Clyde still hadn't heard from her. He wondered if that was Jerry's doing—or worse, maybe Ayana also believed that the name DJ Clydoscope would be kryptonite for her career.

This wasn't the first time someone had pulled back from him the moment they fully grasped who he was, either. In just a few short weeks, several lively conversations with a potential collaborator had gone ice cold after "Fly So High" came up.

Stranger still, Clyde suddenly realized, was that almost every person who turned away was black. Meanwhile, any number of white industry folks were more than willing to schmooze and pose for pictures...

Why were the brothers and sisters hesitant to associate with him? Several months ago, at the height of his song's popularity, Clyde was hip-hop's darling from coast to coast. Could it be that since the HRA was back on its feet, Afrigro-Americans just wanted to keep a good thing going for as long as possible?

It wasn't as if the government had made any sweeping policy changes in response to his song. All they did later on was arrest a bunch of people involved with the SOJ hack, then got back to business as usual—while of course giving the usual reassurances that the system was secure and people's privacy was safe.

Clyde supposed that today, people regarded his song as merely a puff of smoke that had dissipated into nothingness. His cries for help from the heart of the inner city were irrelevant and forgotten, now that the president had been re-elected and MARVIN was fully operational again. Except that Clyde was very far away from Newark, soaking up the Los Angeles energy thanks to Eddie Pryor's persistent recruiting efforts—and Caucs seemed to be the only people who wanted him around.

What could that possibly mean? Did they *really* like his lyrics and think he had talent with long-term potential? Or did he just fill one black slot in their diverse roster of artists, like a Hollywood-style investment portfolio? Nolan would probably agree with that take. But still, his old mentor had also been one of the loudest voices encouraging him to leave town and give LA a shot.

Clyde got a bit of a sinking feeling as he thought about home. Because he hadn't simply *left* his old neighborhood, but *escaped* it. Run away from violence and mistrust and self-destruction—right into the arms of an entertainment mecca run by white people.

That was the trade-off he had agreed to. Leaning on Caucs for safety and the opportunity to grow his career into something that would last. But he still couldn't see what they wanted from *him*, and it was stressing him out! Was the plan just to make a few bucks off the last of his name recognition for a year or two, before dropping him back into obscurity once the well ran dry? Or worse, were they using him as a prop to show the world that 'I have black friends,' 'I support the black community'?

Clyde found this kind of thinking very unpleasant. "Fly So High" had been pure, an idealistic plea made in good faith. And he'd gotten what he envisioned, fame and fortune and doors opening with the red carpet rolled out. But less than a year into the whole process, and already he was becoming aware of a different kind of darkness within this glitzy world of success.

Even more confusing, Clyde sensed that of all the people he had met on this journey out west, it was Eddie Pryor, with his shifty grin and wiggling mustache, who he could trust the most.

He closed his eyes and tried to enjoy this calm afternoon on the patio. Later tonight he would be out socializing again, this time mingling at some art gallery opening. There was no telling who might be angling toward him hungrily—or slinking away in fright.

24. THE WORST MOTIVATOR

"Excuse me, Your Prescience. I hate to disturb you so soon after everything you've been through, but I feel that I must."

Emissary Karlov closed his eyes and gave a slight bow. The bulky man then took a few steps back.

The Prescient One lay on his divan, weary but also joyful to be back in his inner sanctum. The bombed-out chambers had been rebuilt during his absence. Now he was resting after the spectacular return reception he had received while touring the Mall of Absolution earlier in the day.

"It's no trouble, Samuel," he said. "Whatever's on your mind. Let us speak man to man."

Karlov smiled happily for a moment, then his face sobered as he reached into his attaché case and removed a tablet. He tapped the screen several times before handing it over.

"No doubt you will want a full briefing on the state of our mini-nation. Thankfully, I can report that once the initial panic surrounding your abduction subsided, this Modestian family rallied together in ways that would have made you very proud. But—"

"But," the Prescient One said, "what I see here does not look good at all."

"Ah, no, Your Prescience. How best shall I put it? Our church continues to grow as the alternative way of life we offer becomes more widely known. And, after the first Sentinels of Jubilee hack in October, we easily absorbed that first wave of techno-refugees. However, as you now grasp…"

The Prescient One had been watching a montage of footage compiled from the Mall's security network. There were instances of theft inside several storefronts, acts of lewd behavior in dark corners, and worst of all, physical altercations on the auxiliary property outside the main structure. Here steel dormitories had been hastily built to accommodate the additional refugees, many of whom were not equipped to endure the cold Minnesota winter months once the church had reached capacity.

The Prescient One handed the device back and said, "That's enough. Please continue."

"An unfortunate development, to be sure," Karlov said. "But I don't think anyone can be blamed. Had *you* been here during that time, perhaps the result would still be the same. And Mod knows, our longstanding members have done everything they could to be welcoming. The plain fact is that not all of the newcomers are acting in good faith."

"Then we have several challenges to address. First and foremost, we must *defend* the church. Our people and our way of life are why the Mall became a destination, or target, in the first place."

"Yes, yes. Naturally."

"Next, for violations rooted in carelessness or

ignorance about our customs, I suggest firm but forgiving enforcement. Finally, zero tolerance for any and all *malicious* behavior. We cannot let predators think they've found a new group of pushovers to fleece, by using our hearts against us with sentimental pleas."

"Strength, not weakness. I understand."

The Prescient One rose from the divan and walked a slow circle around the room. He said, "But there's also the matter of their sheer numbers. How many arrived in total?"

Karlov looked up at the ceiling. "Off the top of my head… In October, seven hundred people came, and all settled inside the main Mall complex. Starting in November the numbers ballooned, and I believe an additional fifteen hundred arrived. Thank Mod we allocated the resources to build the necessary structures so no one froze to death! Anyhow, in December the numbers dropped—whether due to your, uh… absence or because the Holy Holidays were approaching, I do not know. Still, nearly four hundred more came. Estimates for the first half of this month are approximately one hundred."

"We could be looking at three thousand in all by the end of January," the church leader marveled. "That's a quarter of our own membership here at home, not even including those who attend independent churches throughout the country. For us to absorb that many new people, coming from all backgrounds and having different motivations… And not just to provide food and housing, but allegedly to teach them the ways of our religion, which itself is still so young and in development… Emissary Karlov, I don't see how we can manage it without losing ourselves. Basic accommodation might be doable, but only if we quarantined all of the refugees while screening for authentic converts."

"Yes and no, Your Prescience. Already a number of the troublemakers have invoked their human rights in an attempt to avoid punishment for their mischief. And several lawyers within the refugee ranks have jumped to their defense. It is quite distressing."

"But of course!" the Prescient One said with a wry laugh. "It takes two to tango. But this actually relates to another point I want to make. Emissary, our faith is not yet set in stone. The true believers are doing glorious work hammering out the fine details in the mapmaking sessions. What if impostors were to barge in and start polluting those holy waters? No! We *cannot* allow our charitable instincts to be taken advantage of to the point that the structural integrity of our community is put in danger."

Karlov shuddered. He had never seen the Prescient One so angry before. "What do you propose?"

"We can't possibly interview them all face to face. Besides, sometimes judging a person's character is more subjective than we'd like to believe. So we must test their purported faith instead. Tempt them. Let them reveal their true natures. They will either find a home with us… or be asked to move along."

"What kind of tests, Your Prescience?"

"We have thousands of cameras in place, do we not? Our own little surveillance fiefdom, haha. Surely you and the other emissaries can arrange a series of real-world situations to draw out the best and worst of our refugee population."

"Very good. And to think, if even only a third of them pass muster, it would mean an additional thousand new Modestians!"

"Perhaps." The Prescient One raised a finger. "Better that we reject all but a hundred, if their hearts aren't true. Remember, while the church itself was initially founded on reactionary principles, its long-term survival depends on beliefs that have the capacity to *grow*. Fear is the worst motivator when making any decision. So, my friend, you must challenge the newcomers to surmount their weaknesses. Then they won't have to deny their essence while assimilating into our flock."

"You are a wise man, truly." As Emissary Karlov turned away, he paused and said, "If you are not too fatigued, I have one last question."

"Of course, Samuel. What is it?"

"Before your unfortunate ordeal, you had mentioned to me in private discussion the need to dive deep and explore the source of what created you, as well as the man Scott Cullen beforehand. I wonder if your recent experiences served to shed any light on the matter?"

The Prescient One nodded. "Blindingly so. And I am still… reacting. Please give me time to make sense of it all, then I promise to incorporate new wisdom that might help enrich our church."

"Indeed, Your Prescience. It is my honor to serve Mod, and act as your confidante when needed. Rest well…"

25. A MAYPOLE IN BROOKLYN

"Yeah, I can manage this."

Chris Donohugh rubbed his hands together briefly, then began moving down the sidewalk with the two Corgis scuttling alongside. A brief reprieve from the winter chill had brought many New Yorkers out on this bright, cloudless Saturday. He and Kate stopped in at their favorite neighborhood coffee shop, then began a relaxing stroll around the Brooklyn streets.

"So," he said, "this is the life, eh?"

"We're doin' it. Everything's back to normal. Well —for us, at least. Any updates on… ?"

"Not yet. But damn, the concert is getting a lot of coverage."

"Still?"

"Oh yeah. Even some sites over in the UK and Germany."

"Uh-oh," Kate said with a laugh. "This could get out of control."

"Effing Glenn, man. That guy is a human battering ram."

"If all you have is a hammer, everything looks like a nail…"

"Hammer of justice!"

Chris handed off the leashes and started playing air guitar. Kate waited patiently. This was just one of the quirks she'd had to accept about her musician husband. By the time he concluded his faux-solo with a leap, her attention was already elsewhere.

"You hungry?" she asked while trailing after the dogs, who smelled something tasty in the air and were moving forward aggressively. "Annnd," she called back to him, "looks like it's early enough that the wait won't be too long."

Chris caught up to her and they took their place in line on the sidewalk outside of Blockbuster Tacos. He craned his neck to get a better view of the crowd, judging that it would only be twenty minutes until they ordered.

Just then a pair of mini-drones appeared at the nearby intersection. One peeled off toward them and slowly made its way down the street, then zipped away.

"What the hell was that all about?" Chris said.

"Beats me."

"Like, I *never* see those things flying around here."

"Oh well," Kate sighed. "The new normal, I guess."

"Yeah, yeah. Another thing we're supposed to accept without being told about first."

"Don't start on that now, babe. 'Cause remember, I married the *guitarist*, not the singer."

"So just shut up and look good?"

"Basically." She slipped her arm into his.

The line crept forward. The dogs made friends with a chocolate Labrador whose owner was several places behind, so the Donohughs stepped back and talked to her while they waited to order.

Inside the restaurant's seating area, they ended up joining the other woman at one of the long picnic tables. She was a Pilates instructor named Laurie, who promised Kate a free session at her studio that was in the neighborhood. While they chatted, the dogs played cleanup crew underneath the table, snorting greedily and gobbling up bits of food that had fallen onto the floor. After an exchange of phone numbers, Laurie gave Kate and Chris a quick hug and then went power-walking away as her Lab trotted along.

"Back home," Chris said, "or onward?"

"Let's keep going. Work off this meal."

"You lead the way. Or… maybe they will."

The Corgis were in pursuit of a new scent. They lurched left at the next corner and pawed forward until the trail went cold on a front stoop halfway down the block.

"So, do you think he did it?"

Chris froze. She had finally broached the subject. After weeks of tranquility and renewed wedded bliss following Kate's return from overseas HRA duty, here it was. The test he dreaded. It had the power to tear his world apart forever.

He said, "How would *you* feel if it was all true, what they're saying about him?"

"I really don't know." Kate tugged at one of her knit gloves. "Because I just don't understand."

"What, exactly? Glenn himself, or what he might've done?"

"Chris, let's just assume he did it, that he was part of the SOJ. *And,* what if he was in the right? That would mean I'm one of the bad guys."

"Oh. Meaning you'd also have to ask yourself how and when that happened, right?"

"Yup. Because we all used to be on the same side fighting for the same things. Our methods were different, sure. You guys doing your music, and me working with charities and PACs."

"What was the separation point then?" Chris asked. "That our bands never reached the level of success to become corporate sell-outs? Whereas the HRA—a big government entity—is the equivalent of that in your sphere?"

"But if that's accurate..." Kate trailed off. "Okay, here's the paradox. We've been striving for change our whole lives because we were told that was the thing to do. Then, our generation actually achieves the goal, so we're not just protesting out in the streets anymore. We've got offices, budgets, and infrastructure in place to really go for it. I don't see how that can be a bad thing."

Chris tightened his grip on the leashes as they approached a crosswalk that was on a red light. He said, "Maybe it's got nothing to do with the administration itself. Not the goals or even the people working there, who let's assume—Sentinels sympathizers excluded—are competent and loyal. The bigger point is that *any* company or group of that size, with that much reach... it's vulnerable to... not even corruption or rot, but... Maybe the expectations of the people it's supposed to serve are too high. Or do all entities just automatically become *targets* for those who, I don't know... hate big things, or want to skim off the top? Eh, I've already drifted so far from my original thought here, I don't know where I was going with it."

"Yeah, you touched on a lot," Kate said. "I guess, now that we've been around for a while, people see the HRA as one more government bureaucracy."

"Not only that, your charter really swung for the fences! This wasn't just, say, the Get More People to Eat Healthy Administration. So give yourself a break. It's been a good sprint, a good first round. There's nothing wrong with saying the HRA'll have to adapt, like any business, really."

"Maybe, hmm... But getting back to Glenn. Why would a guy like him join that fight, when there are so many other ills he could've gone after? I mean, *you* saw him back around the end of October. Did he say anything, or did you pick up any hints that maybe something was up with him?"

Chris leaned over and started adjusting one of the dogs' harnesses. He needed to buy some time while figuring out how to deflect her question without telling an outright lie.

"Ah, you know how he is. Goes off on every topic like some conspiracy theorist calling a talk show. '9/11 was an inside job!' 'Why can't civilians explore Antarctica?!' So yeah, he probably said some stuff about the hack too."

"And did you agree with him?"

Chris looked Kate directly in the eyes and said, "And what if I did? What if that song I'm writing right now is called 'Restitution Junkies'? Would you leave me—or throw your panties at me?"

Kate held his stare for a moment. Slowly, their mouths both curled up into a smile. She eased forward and pecked him on the lips.

"You've got me wrapped around your finger, Mr. Donohugh. More than you even realize."

Kate placed a palm onto her stomach and rubbed it in a circle. Her eyes flickered.

"What? You mean… ?"

"Mm-hmm. It's early… but I'm late."

Chris felt his head swoon in a buoyant thrilling rush of incomprehensible emotions. He closed his eyes as enormous tears formed and rolled down his cheeks.

And then they were embracing, rocking back and forth to the silent song that was playing only for them. The Corgis walked a slow circle around their ankles, turning the Donohughs into a maypole lost in a hopeful reverie.

Life was good. And God willing, it was about to get a whole lot better.

26. CARDINAL SIN

"I'm telling you, Reverend, you're being too harsh."

"But it's just tough love," Matthias Witherspoon pleaded. "And if not from me, you're going to hear it from somebody else who's less compassionate and got less skin in the game."

"No, no. That's no excuse for you ridin' the Tinfoil Express."

Nadine Jones folded her arms after she said this, and Matthias noted that several others in attendance were nodding their heads in approval. Before he could respond, another man stood up to speak.

"Look here, Mr. Reverend. I never took sides during all this internal strife been going on these last few months. And I *thought* everything was patched up nice again. But now it looks like you're back at it, frothing in the pulpit again. That wasn't part of the agreement."

Matthias got an uneasy feeling in his stomach. The mood at this Sunday afternoon meeting was starting to turn against him. He wanted to double down, but sensed that it might be wiser to lose the skirmish for diplomacy's sake. Maybe there was a third way…

"Aw, come on now, people," he said, flashing his teeth in a who-me smile. "You know how ol' Matthias can get. Once the engine revs up, sometimes I run it too hot and get hog wild. Hehe, so how about this? Maybe we'll pass out yellow flags, and anyone who sees me get loose can call a penalty, like in football."

A few people snickered. Others were not so impressed by this little joke.

"I'd throw the flag right now," Nadine clucked. "He's just swapping out the business suit for the clown costume. Still the same Witherspoon bag of tricks, though. I've seen it all before."

"That's right, that's right," came the response. "Say it, sister!"

A flustered Matthias switched into humble mode. "Listen, y'all. We been through this before. Times are gonna start getting tougher for black folk, starting last week. So I got to speak on it, is all."

Some murmurs and whispers. He felt like he might eke out a victory after all. But—these people were his flock, not enemies or Joe Public. Simply having this discussion without bruising anyone's ego was a delicate matter.

A younger man stood up. Thin, wearing sharp clothes, and a recent college graduate. He said, "If that's the case, then how can *you* help, dear Reverend? Because I assume what you're referring to falls into the categories of economics and politics. Do you know how to solve those kinds of problems?"

Louder chatter now. Some hesitant applause that might keep feeding on itself if Matthias didn't come back with an effective retort. He raised his arms placatingly.

"I hear you, Mr. Ames. And welcome back home. Congratulations on collecting your diploma last month —was that in three-and-a-half or four-and-a-half years? No doubt you're eager to make your mark on the world. But this youthful enthusiasm to run out and prove yourself, it don't realize something that I do. As a man of God, I understand that the challenges facing us have nothing to do with physically going any*where*. Because the most important battles are fought within." Matthias touched his breast and then his temple. "You got to change here and here, to have any *chance* at protecting yourself."

On-the-fence grumbles and a couple of meek boos came back at him from the seated crowd. The young man said, "But we need *practical steps* to take, so we can start seeing results in our daily lives. We have real dreams. And no time to sit around day*dreaming!*"

"Preach on!" someone shouted. "Oh yes, the Reverend has met his match!"

Witherspoon said, "My man. We are taking steps. Community investment. Got the new farmers market starting up in the spring. Youth crime intervention programs. Do you—"

"That's small potatoes," Ames interrupted. "Or reacting to a problem that's already there. People, I get what the Reverend's been hinting at. If the HRA pulls back, then the vultures are gonna fly in. Koreans, Indians, Russians, Israelis, whoever! And we know them immigrants don't care about us. They'll just say, 'I'm here too. So whatcha gonna do?' Any thoughts on that, Matthias?"

"Of course, you're right. All the groups you mentioned, plus the Armenians, the Vietnamese, the Salvadorans, and more. They're all here and they want to be heard. Their grievance, their glory, their power play. So, who gets priority seating at that crowded table? Not you! But I got a little secret to share—it's all gonna blow up in everyone's face, yessir. 'Cause MARVIN won't stop, *can't* stop. He'll be happy to oblige some first-generation Syrian refugee, who says that Turkey or Iraq blew up his house. Then the chant will be, '*Pay* me too!' Yup, the whole world is comin' here to get paid. And our country's just one big strip-mining club, makin' it rain for everyone, hahahaha!"

Ames threw his arms out violently, then wagged a stern finger to prevent the room from exploding into chaos. He said, "Even if that's all true and our dear leader can see into the future, the fact remains, ladies and gentlemen. Mr. Witherspoon *ain't... got... no... plan.* He's a scaremonger, a band-aid seller. At the end of the day, he simply lacks the tools or the ability required to fight off the coming storm. A Noah he is not!"

And right in that moment, Matthias Witherspoon felt his world come crashing down. Young Robert Ames, who had grown up attending Sunday services at his church, in the course of a diatribe which borrowed from his own pulpit style, had exposed a fatal weakness.

Because faith didn't read the newspaper or put food on people's tables. It was there to help a person absorb life's defeats and still get out of bed in the morning. But it couldn't pick you a winner in the stock market, or resist the encroaching repercussions of an immigration policy which had kicked Afrigro-Americans to the back of the bus.

As if Reparations was the final smokescreen after sixty years of open borders, and soon Heritage Americans, black and white alike, would find themselves electorally swamped by their imported neighbors. Their own happiness, preferences, communities, and right to self-determination were null and void—because long ago, a political decision had been made to change the demographic makeup of an entire landmass.

The United States of America as it had been known for centuries was no more. Transformed in the blink of an eye without consulting anyone, let alone by royal decree. And the people being overrun were expected not to mourn the loss of their homeland, but just roll over and fade away. Never mind that it was their own families who were responsible for creating *this* nice place, where so many others from around the world wanted to live...

Matthias snapped back into the moment. He realized with sick clarity that the crisis playing out was a mess of his own making. Because in warning of particular dangers that he as church leader couldn't defend against, he had committed the salesman's cardinal sin. And now his followers, truly aware of the real-world peril they faced, would begin looking for answers elsewhere.

He fumbled for the kerchief in his pocket and wiped his face. Robert Ames was smiling in triumph as he received pats on the back from the other parishioners. Reverend Witherspoon gathered himself to utter the words that would bring this meeting to a close as quickly as possible.

There was no use prolonging his opponents' satisfaction, now that he had lost.

27. TICKING TIME CAPSULE

The banging of hammers resonated throughout the entire structure. Drills whirred and buzzed every few seconds. Sam Cooke was crooning from a speaker on the upstairs landing.

President Eileen Jeffries-Lao stood smiling, drywall saw in hand, while several members of the press corps snapped photos of her and an assembled crew of Minorican volunteers. After the workers returned to their tasks, Eileen pulled off her gloves and attempted to brush the construction dust out of her hair. She removed her yellow-tinted goggles and handed them to one of the organizers as she stepped out into the front yard.

"Nice outfit," Vice President Hank Pendleton said, motioning to the beige canvas overalls Eileen had been provided earlier in the day. The big Texan was wearing his own personal outfit of buffalo plaid flannel shirt and black stonewashed jeans.

"Tools of the trade," she replied. "Are you lollygagging around or what?" She smiled as she spoke, aware that there were press photographers crawling all over the site of this halfway house which they were helping to renovate.

Hank pointed up toward the roof. "See that gutter? Rusted and rotten. It's got to be replaced. I'm just waiting on a ladder that's tall enough so I can start ripping it down."

Eileen nodded at Hank's Secret Service detail. "Are they really going to let you climb up there? You'd be quite the sitting duck, a mighty fine target."

"*Someone's* had her coffee this morning," the vice president said to one of his minders. "Come on, back to work…"

An hour later, Eileen was on the move as part of a caravan that would visit a number of locations around the DC area to commemorate Martin Luther King Jr. Day. The TV in her limousine showed one of the many parades that were taking place across the country. On screen, a troupe of black high schoolers wearing the bright outfits of a marching band proceeded down the street in unison. Business as usual—all was well on this annual celebration of Dr. King's life.

Eileen fished out a metal flask from inside her handbag and took a sip. It had been *cold* in that house, with all the doors being left open so workers could come and go freely. Now she was off to a shelter to ladle out meals, before getting herself cleaned up to attend the headstone unveiling ceremony for a Baltimore civil rights leader who had recently passed away.

It was a grind of a day to start the week of her inaugural festivities, but nothing so stressful as the lead-up to this holiday two years ago. Because of all the historical bills that had come due during her first term in office, perhaps none were as potentially explosive as the ticking time capsule that was the sealed MLK archives.

Back in 1977, a judge had decreed that many documents surrounding King's life and death, including the government's full-court press of surveillance as approved by FBI Director J. Edgar Hoover, should be kept under lock and key for fifty years. Eileen Jeffries-Lao happened to occupy the Oval Office when this vault was scheduled for exposure to disinfecting sunlight—and much public scrutiny.

A considerable number of these pages had already leaked out over the years, however, which not only cast a dark shadow on King's personal reputation, but also raised questions about the government's official narrative of the events surrounding his assassination. President Jeffries-Lao believed it would be reckless to permit an unvarnished data dump of the remainder.

Instead, her administration had quietly invited a group of prominent Afrigro-American leaders to meet with representatives from several alphabet agencies for a private game of poker one evening in the fall of 2026. Papers were spread out across an enormous conference table. The two parties then engaged in a tense showdown, before each side selected an equal quantity of undesirable items to be destroyed—and thus lost to history for all time.

A sizable trove of salacious or otherwise troubling material remained in the mix, to help ward off potential accusations of a cover-up once the public was granted full access to the files.

The location of that secret meeting had been a clean room. No cameras. No electronic devices of any kind permitted. No MARVIN.

And so now in January of 2029, the initial fervor surrounding the archives' release having long since died down, the best of the legacy of the man named *Martin* lived on.

The presidential limousine eased into a parking lot where law enforcement and reporters had gathered in anticipation of Eileen's arrival. She popped a breath mint to mask any lingering traces of alcohol, then closed her handbag and waited for the car to stop.

All she needed to do for the rest of the day was go through the motions with a smile on her face. Because in less than a week, Eileen Jeffries-Lao would be sworn in for her second term as president. Then she would be truly free to use the full force of the United States government—FBI included—to see to it that her agenda moved forward at an aggressive pace.

28. FEW KNOW MY NAME

"Clyde, goddammit, I brought you out here so your star could shine. Now don't get me wrong, I knew from before day one that there might be some, uh… if not diva moments, let's say principled outbursts. But Jesus Christ, this?! What the hell, bud?"

Clyde Jenkins had never seen Eddie Pryor mad before. Like, for real mad, and not just playing it up in a meeting to get what he wanted.

"I'm sorry, Mr. Pryor. Honestly, I—"

"Don't gimme any of that hangdog shit, please. I've had a hell of a time cleaning up your mess. What I really need right now is a drink, and some silence."

"Oh."

"Yeah, 'cause I gotta *think*. About how to fix those burned bridges… maybe even flip the situation around… so everything ends up better than before. Ooh, baby! That's why they call me Eddie P.! The cooker, the cleaner, the clairvoyant dream weaver. I have touched *billions* of hearts around the world, and yet few know my name. Oh, you like that, do ya?"

Clyde watched Eddie dance a little jig as he mixed a drink at the wet bar here in the man's downstairs den.

He himself had been brought here by an unmarked LAPD vehicle just a short while ago. He'd seen Eddie hand the two officers something while slinking into the house, and then waited while the men talked outside for several minutes. He tried to smile now that Eddie was in a better mood.

"You don't realize the kind of influence I have, kid." Eddie waltzed over to his recliner, artfully brushing away the bottom of his satin robe before plopping down and kicking up his feet. "But it's true. Of all the showbiz heroes the average person worships, I bet you that I've had a hand in one or two of their careers. Like... you know the flick *Unstoppable Memphis* about that old rap group?"

"Of course," Clyde said. "Been listening to those dudes forever."

"Yeah, well, I rewrote half the damn script for them —*uncredited*, mind you. No one puts *me* on camera. No one hands *me* the microphone. Because..." Eddie waved a hand up and down the length of his body. "Which is fine, because I do my best work behind the scenes. Making things happen! The sizzle on Hollywood's grill!"

"Eddie's empire, it sounds like."

"Exactly! Which is why... you are driving me *insane*, Clyde! The way I see it, all we gotta do is figure out how to work your integrity angle into my proven system—and we'll make you a freaking *legend!*"

"Legendary status, alright!" Clyde pumped his fist.

The muscles on Eddie's face collapsed. He pushed the recliner down with his feet and leaned forward. "But I can't do it when I get a phone call in the middle of the night, saying that my newest protégé snuck onto the property where Miss Ayana McGinn lives *with her parents*, and darn near got himself killed trying to do some romantic-movie bullshit outside her window. Do you see how that might concern me?"

Clyde got up from the sofa and went to the bar. Dejectedly, he dropped several ice cubes into a glass, then poured soda over top. The fizz bounced against his cheeks as he took a sip. Finally, he said, "I know, Eddie. It's just... I need to... I don't know how to say it."

Pryor's expression softened as he said, "Help me understand what's going on."

Clyde sat down again and rubbed the side of his head with his palm. "I'm the new kid in town. And I like this girl. A lot! But damn, it seems like right from the start, a lot of people be tellin' me no."

"Uh-huh. Go on."

"And part of me knows I'm a fluke. I got like, stupid lucky when 'Fly So High' took off. It changed everything *for* me—but not *about* me. Now I see that maybe not everyone out here all that impressed by DJC, neither. Okay, so what I'm supposed to do? Got to step up, that's what. Assert myself, prove I belong. That I ain't, like, some pretender out of his league. But... maybe I am?"

Eddie stood up. His eyes were glassy. "Come here, son. That was just... from the heart. We need more of that in this town."

Clyde set his drink aside and joined Eddie for a hug. He heard himself sniffle and then dropped his face onto Eddie's shoulder. He pulled away, shuddering slightly as he wiped under his eyes and said, "God damn."

After a silent moment, Eddie said, "You're a good kid, Clyde. And I know I get ridiculous sometimes, but this city can do that to ya. You have my promise on two things. One, I will never tell a soul what you just shared with me. So unless you wanna express that in one of your songs, it will remain private."

"Thank you, Eddie."

"And as for your shenanigans up at the McGinn residence tonight… While I can't guarantee that no one will ever know, rest assured my team has been out there trying to cover your tracks since the moment I got the call."

"Oh yeah?" Clyde looked up. "So no tabloid stuff?"

"Any and all visual evidence we can acquire will be purchased and destroyed. Then it'll just be he said, she said. And I highly doubt the ambitious young Miss McGinn wants any bad press either, now that she's trying to be a *serious* actress."

"Oh my goodness, Eddie, you saved my life! How much do I owe you for buying up them pictures?"

"Not one cent."

"No! Why?!"

"Because now you know I'm not just all talk. I've got your back when it counts. That's a fair price to pay."

Clyde exhaled with happy relief. He said, "One thing, though. How'd you get your people on the case so quick? Were you, uh… waiting for me to mess up?"

Eddie flashed a smile. "Clyde Jenkins, you are *not* the first entertainer under my tutelage to make a damn fool of himself. Looking out for the team's interests is just like an insurance policy. Yep, Eddie P. has all the bases covered!"

"Alright then, cool. Should I catch a ride home, or… ?"

Eddie waved a hand. "There's two spare bedrooms down the hall. Go get some rest, you creepy night prowler! I'll arrange a car in the morning."

"Thanks again."

"Forget it, kid. We're all young once. Even the rich and famous…"

29. CAUSING A RUCKUS

"Murray, let's go."

The metal door clanked open. Two heavily armed prison guards stood outside waiting.

"No cuffs?" Glenn asked.

"Not today," one of the guards said. "Get your shit and come on."

Glenn didn't wait for clarification. Whether he was being rotated to another cell or transferred to a new facility, anything was better than stewing in this six-by-eight concrete pen which was slowly driving him insane. He quickly grabbed a few personal items and exited the cell.

He walked slowly down the corridor. The guard behind him held a heavy baton at the ready. They passed through several remotely activated door locks, then stepped into an elevator.

On the ride up, one of the guards held out a mesh knapsack and said, "Put it all in here."

Glenn deposited his belongings, then awaited further instructions. The elevator doors opened onto a hallway that was more welcoming than the austere passageways below, and the guards nudged him in the direction of a large office.

"Inmate G. Murray here to see you, sir," the lead guard announced.

As Glenn entered the room, a man of medium build with leathery skin rose from his chair behind a heavy old desk. He motioned in front of him and said, "Sit down."

Glenn sat without a word. He had never seen, let alone met this man before, but assumed he was the warden. So Glenn kept his guard up, sensing that his fate hung in the balance.

"Tell me, Mr. Murray," the man drawled, then exhaled heavily through his nostrils. "Would you say that you've been anything less than a model inmate during your time with us?"

"No, sir," Glenn replied. "I haven't been disciplined since I got here."

"Very true." The warden tapped a newspaper that was open in front of him. "But someone's been causing a ruckus about you. Or should I say, a *raucous?*"

The paper was rotated so that Glenn could read it. A finger pointed out the headline that read, "Local Bands Unite in Support of Jailed Singer." He felt a surge of vitality after weeks spent in cold isolation.

"Did you know about this?" the warden asked.

"I—"

"I guess it doesn't really matter. Not now, at least. Shouldn't even be my concern. But what you did…"

"Allegedly." Glenn couldn't help himself. His gusto was returning.

The warden snatched away the newspaper, crushing it with his large hands and dropping the clump into a wastebasket beside him. He said, "Don't make me mad, please. I may not have the power to hold you any longer, but an unfortunate accident might very well befall you on your way out. Understand?"

Glenn nodded.

"I'm gonna speak my mind before you leave us. Don't think it was just your friends that made it happen, neither. These Jeffries-Lao executive orders are really what punched your ticket. Amnesties and pardons for criminal scum across the board. All I know is, you broke the law. And where *I* come from, if such is the case, then a man's got to serve his time."

Glenn said, "Sir, I haven't once seen a lawyer, or been charged with any crime. Is that also how things are done where you come from?"

"Oh, no, most definitely not. But don't you try to pin that on me. I'm just the babysitter. Not my call what time Mommy and Daddy come home."

"Or if the kids sneak out of the house." Glenn stood up and smirked. "Thanks for the hospitality, but the food here stinks. I'm out."

As he left the office, Glenn came face to face with the two guards from earlier. Tall and burly himself, he sized them up without fear, then cracked a smile.

Somehow, some way, he was getting out of lockup. To breathe the fresh free air for the first time in more than six weeks. He couldn't wait to unleash his voice once again.

30. THEY FOUND SOMETHING

Nolan Simmons was not a drinking man. One or two cocktails during the Holy Holidays or when celebrating a milestone, mostly. So when his right-hand-man Damon discovered him swiveling around in an easy chair with a half-empty bottle of whiskey in his lap, he knew something big was up.

"Hey, boss… You, uh, you okay?"

Nolan's droopy eyelids slowly eased open. He said, "Not really. No. But I ain't thirsty!" He raised the bottle. "We got some real trouble on our hands, Dee. And pretty soon, maybe no one's gonna be okay."

Damon pulled up a chair. He pointed at the bottle and said, "Gimme some of that first. Then lay it on me."

"Right. Here, drink up… So last week, I got the tech crew to put out the call for more historical data."

"Yup. I been keepin' tabs on their hours. Go on."

"So first couple days, nothing out of the ordinary. I didn't expect much from overseas that soon anyway. This first push is mainly to get the word out—then we'll start seeing real results a few months down the road."

"Cool, cool."

"As for the domestic side of the search, I couldn't predict what might turn up. 'Cause everything's been sifted over pretty good—or burned—these past few years. I just never..."

Nolan trailed off, his eyes glazing over as he took hold of the bottle again.

Damon said, "What's got you so spooked, boss?"

Nolan whispered, "The Sentinels did a lot more than bury some new code inside MARVIN. *They found something!*"

"And... now you got it too?"

"Yeah. I sure do. But I don't know if I want it."

"What the hell is it, Nolan?"

"Turns out MARVIN—the system's original, pre-hack version—was holding out on us."

"Say what?"

"He held stuff back, by design! Those sneaky mofos over at the HRA were hiding *their own cache* of inconvenient archives!"

"You mean... bad stuff *we* did?"

"Hehe, well... It sure makes things look a lot grayer. Especially 'cause the HRA has been all about moving the green from white hands to black."

Damon brought his fingertips together. Slowly, he said, "So whatchu worried about more—that we'll have to pay some of the money we got back, or are we gonna owe a lot more on top of that?"

"I like the way you think," Nolan said, now perking up. "But it's even more complicated than what you're talking about. Since we know the HRA wants to expand into other countries, here's what I think happened. While they were helping set things up, someone must've noticed that a lot of the documents they were feeding into the other MARVINs... Well, that stuff actually brushes up against people here at home too."

"Yeah, I guess that makes sense. Like, can't only be everyone moves *north*, right?"

"No doubt. So they've been gathering data on all the races, from lotsa different countries, and *I suspect* they got overwhelmed. Because history is just too damn complex, man. As for our buddy MARVIN... Well, he's constipated now!"

They burst out laughing. The bottle got passed back to Damon as he said, "So if they already having problems just trying to add a couple more countries— uh, real quick, can you say which ones?"

"Colombia and Aruba, I know for sure. Then there's a couple of British colonies. My hunch says, one dip of the toe and they freaked the hell out. Decided to back off for a while."

Damon said, "Maybe they just need more computing power?"

"Haha, nice try, Dee. But no. It's like they realize if they keep going, the blame won't always be white, white, white. So they're backpedaling, trying to press stop without anybody knowing. Look at it this way. How many Aztec types you think maybe owned some Africans down there? Or vice versa?"

"Oh... crap. So we might have to start cashin' out *other people* besides Caucs?"

"Now you're getting it! And going one step further, what gives the government the right to hold anything back? Should be, you find it, you post it. So now, here's a little theory. MARVIN ain't human, right? His goal is complete and objective historical accuracy. What happens if you hide stuff from him or refuse to announce his verdict? Say he's tied in to the drone network that's got law enforcement powers—that could mean some serious robot apocalypse shit!"

"We're gonna need another bottle, you keep talkin' like that," Damon said. "But seriously, what else about that keepin' secrets part bothers you?"

Nolan took a moment to calm himself. Then he said, "The fact they're picking and choosing which archives to share, to me that looks like it could have legal ramifications. Meaning… Okay, you may not remember this, but back around ten years ago, this undocumented guy—we're talkin' pre-amnesty now—he dragged this white girl who was out jogging in sexy pants into the bushes and did his thing. Then he chopped her up and buried her in garbage bags, like it was nothin'!"

"Jesus…"

"Yup, yup. Anyhow, cops messed up when they arrested the cat and so he walked on a technicality. Right on back to Mexico, safe and sound!"

"Son of a bitch! But what's that got to do with…"

"Courtroom complexities, my friend. There's a whole squadron of lawyers who been takin' little ankle bites out of the HRA this whole time, just slowly chipping away at the thing. But so far, they ain't scored any direct hits. Well, this treasure trove I got might give 'em enough ammo to tear off the whole head!"

Damon exhaled a long, slow breath. "Oh. Now I see."

"You do? That's great. What's our best course of action?"

"No, no. What I mean is, now I see why you're sitting by yourself drinking all that whiskey."

"Sittin' on top of a powder keg is what I'm doing."

"Can't stay there forever. Otherwise… what if one of our tech boys accidentally sends something out, because he doesn't understand what it is?"

"Oh my god!" Nolan leaped out of his chair—the room did not explode—and wagged a finger at Damon. "I gotta lock this place down!"

31. THE THOUSAND PROBLEMS

Marcus Young found himself pulling lighter duty on Tuesday. The District of Columbia was crawling with Feds like him, so headquarters rotated them through low- and high-priority targets in order to keep everyone fresh and on their toes.

Today a group calling itself Beyond Latiz was hosting an indigenous pride festival inside the National Museum of the American Indian. Several well-known actors and musicians were scheduled to appear, so security had been beefed up slightly to include members of Marcus's FBI team.

They circulated around the museum, pausing now and again to chat with officers from the Metro Police who were also on duty. In addition to the permanent installations, Marcus passed dancers wearing traditional costumes performing in the main atrium, authentic food selections, handmade pottery and crafts for sale, and artists who painted ornate designs on patrons' arms and faces.

Guest lecturers presented their work throughout the

day in the first-floor theater. Topics listed on a large placard outside ranged from a discussion of sacred rituals to how modernity was encroaching upon remote tribes. Marcus listened in on each presentation for a few minutes while making his rounds through the museum's four levels.

He had just re-entered this auditorium when a new speaker took to the stage. The man wore a striped pullover sweater in native pattern and blue jeans accented by large metal belt buckle. An enormous papier mâché pyramid stood next to the lectern, and further away an Uncle Sam piñata dangled from the branches of a plastic tree.

Marcus decided to linger as long as possible to see where this speech might be headed.

"Good afternoon," the man said. "My name is Elias Topiltzin Alhambra. I am currently a professor of trans-hemispheric studies and pan-tribal languages at UC Santa Cruz in California. Prior to that, I spent nearly fifteen years living among my ancestral cousins, the native peoples of Central and South America.

"Today I pose a challenge for Caucasians who talk incessantly about wanting to preserve their heritage. Tell me, what is there worth saving, let alone celebrating? What is the point of building walls, when you only end up locking progress out? Do you do it for your warmongering military-industrial complex, which uses sentimental manipulations to fool you into invading far-away nations?

"Or is it your culture of sickness you defend—the processed food and pharmaceutical cartels that are more interested in paperwork and patents than health? Is it your financial system, which first imposes taxes, then creates investment funds so that you may avoid these taxes, but all the while the money printing machine ensures that inflation prevents you from ever getting ahead?

"I could go on and on, providing countless examples of how your country has not merely failed you, but was meticulously designed to extract the most effort out of its deluded human livestock. Vanity, obesity, ignorance, cruelty, exploitation, and slavery—all dressed up as opportunity. But why listen to me? I am merely an indigenous voice trapped inside occupied lands.

"We native people have been unwilling investors in the half-millennium of bloody schemes that preceded the creation of the skyscraper. On behalf of those who have no voice, I declare that the funding for all modern inventions has come from New World suffering!

"You invaders must finally admit the brutality of your past. Acknowledge that we were not mere primitives. Confess that it was the colonizers' own impatience and unwillingness to understand which resulted in our so-called esoteric wisdom being lost. *You* were the savages in spirit, despite your shiny armor. *We* lived in harmony with our world before you despoiled it.

"Behold the verdict, the referendum on your long and painful rule: the rivers overflow with plastic trash, yet you dare to mock us for our piles of skulls! What a mess you have made of the world which you deign to oversee. How many cities leveled, how many millions of lives lost during your centuries of warfare? How many modern 'crises of diversity' are in fact a direct result of these destabilization campaigns which turned entire populations of innocents into refugees?

"If your civilization feels like it is being ripped apart from within, then blame yourselves for creating a Tower of Babel in every city. Your greed, your shortsighted expediency… all have contributed to your imminent downfall.

"We of the rainforests and the mesas shall survive

while you consume yourselves in an avalanche of hate. For we are the strong ones. The patient. The timeless. The mountain people who were not tempted to forsake our marriage to the steppes for your coins or comforts. We who live along the water's edge, the harsh plains, the mysterious caves...

"We are the true caretakers of this Earth, our spirit eternally striving but never foolhardy. Whereas you— the eternal colonizer—you are desperate to escape this world which you have polluted beyond repair. We wish you not luck but good riddance. And if we hope you succeed, it is only so that you will leave us in peace as you ruin the other wandering stars that populate our beautiful night sky.

"Oh, blessed gods and goddesses, please hear our prayers as we speak from genuine hearts. Protect us from these modern barbarians, who think that their fancy words and overwhelming legal documents can fool the Great Spirits. Shield us from their factory exhaust, the provocative filth that they call entertainment, and the medicines which kill so many of their own each year.

"Do not let our eyes be fooled by the thousand problems hidden within each solution they offer to sell us—for that is their Trojan Horse! Defend us from chasing after their impossible pleasures, and the corrupt path which ends at the tragic cliffs of barrenness. Oh yes, lead us not into temptation, indeed!"

The professor held out his arm in the direction of his props. He said, "We built thousands of pyramids as sacred temples. You obeyed the government-approved food pyramid, and it has become the tomb of entire generations. Now I will repay your haughty Uncle Sam for all that he has done to you, as well as inflicted upon the world..."

Alhambra stepped behind the fake pyramid and

reached down. A moment later, he held a wooden baseball bat aloft.

In a flash, Marcus felt himself hurtling toward the stage. He sprinted down the aisle faster than he ever ran trying to beat out a bunt at first base. Now he plowed full-force into the man in gray who had left his seat and charged the stage shouting obscenities.

They tumbled and rolled in a chaotic stalemate. Finally, Marcus maneuvered the would-be attacker onto his stomach, pinning his arms back just as other officers arrived to complete the submission and apply handcuffs.

As the commotion died down in the auditorium, Professor Alhambra approached Marcus with a grateful smile.

"Thank you very much for defending this event, Officer… ?"

"Young. Special Agent Young."

"Oh. With the FBI? Nice of you to actually *help* an indigenous person for once."

"Say," Marcus said, nodding at the baseball bat. "Were you going to use that on the piñata?"

The professor smirked. "But of course. It was my grand finale."

"What's inside?"

"Ethically grown chocolate candy purchased from farmers who respect the Amazon rainforest. If you'd like, I can still…"

Marcus reached out and grabbed the bat by its head. He tugged until Professor Alhambra released the handle.

"Well, in that case, Mr. Young, be my guest. Batter up!"

"No, that's taking it too far. *Speak* all you want, but don't disrespect the game."

Marcus walked off the stage with a confident strut, knowing that he had done his job. The professor, and the Louisville Slugger, were both safe.

32. WORD TO THE WISE

"I told y'all, the well is dryin' up."

"Easy for you to say."

Dawna Jenkins adjusted her weight forward. "And what's that supposed to mean, Mrs. Thomas?"

The woman seated across the round table said, "That maybe you got another well of your own set up already."

"Yeah," the third woman in the group added. "One that's all filled up 'cause it double dipped in the Reparations trough."

Dawna dropped her hand of playing cards onto the table. She said, "My, my. Just listen to you two today. Who needs enemies when you got friends like these? Any other comments?"

Mrs. Thomas inspected her fanned cards as she said, "How's your boy doing out in Los Angeles, by the way? He meet any movie stars yet?"

"We all had a very nice visit with him, thank you for asking. And what of it if he *has* rubbed shoulders with some celebrities? Is that alright with everyone?"

"Just making conversation, is all. Rita, I'm dumping

two. Deal me, please."

The third woman dealt Mrs. Thomas fresh cards for her cast-offs, then added, "Don't get so touchy now, Dawna. We're just messin' witchu, like we always been doin' with each other. You ain't too fancy for your old friends, are you?"

Dawna picked up her cards. "Okay, then. I love you too. But what I said before was true—and it wasn't 'cause I was bragging or nothin'. I got it on good authority that we need to watch out for ourselves."

"Who said?!" the two other women demanded.

"That, I am not at liberty to discuss. But he—or she—came to me to share what they had discovered."

"And?" Rita asked.

"Just for me to start spreading the word. Because my gossip turns into *our* gossip, which turns into a whole lotta hens sharing the message. So here goes. Reparations as we've known it for the past three years gonna be different in the future."

"Go on."

"And since they started by helping us, there's no way it'll get any better after the change. So we got to prepare for when we get less."

"Less money?" Thomas said.

"That, or maybe less attention. Fewer opportunities, less accommodation. Plus, that's just on the front end!"

"Hold up, woman. The HRA gonna downsize just like that? I don't see how, or why. They makin' money. Lots of jobs in it, for *them*."

"Because," Dawna said, "they're not closing up shop at all. They're just looking away, adjusting their camera."

"To focus on what?"

"Not us! That's all I know, and it's probably all we *need* to know. Because for whatever reason, the government is moving on to something—or someone—else."

"I blame that bitch Lao," Rita said. "Soon as she got herself re-elected, probably told her people to drop us *that night!* And who knows, maybe she was even in on the hack."

"Oh, you must be playin' games now," Thomas said. "Because for a second, you had me nodding right along with you. Too bad you let your mouth keep runnin' into crazy town."

"Me, the crazy talker? What about Dawna? She the one who started this whole thing."

"That's right! So what you got to tell us about the back end of all this, Mizz Jenkins?"

"Same source," Dawna began, "but now maybe with less concrete… not information, but predictions. Basically, think beyond the fact the HRA's gonna set up shop in new places. My friend also worries about the wild card. If the unexpected were to happen."

"Keep going," Thomas said as she shuffled the deck.

"The program almost collapsed because their computers got broken into, right? Well, that's not the only way they could lose control. Like, what if MARVIN doesn't do what they want him to do anymore? Or worse, maybe he starts going in the opposite direction. What you think about that, ladies?"

"The opposite?"

Rita added, "Like come after us? Make *us* pay?"

"Could be!" Dawna said.

"Now who's in crazy town?"

"Just a word to the wise, is all I'm sayin'."

Mrs. Thomas said, "Well, what are we supposed to do if it's gonna turn into a big bother? Please, we need some answers, or direction. Tell us what you would do."

"Or your friend," Rita muttered.

Dawna rose from her seat. "Okay, I've got some thoughts. But first, someone deal these cards while I fetch the iced tea…"

33. PERHAPS ONE DAY

People gasped throughout the corridor. Then they separated and slowly backed toward the walls as he passed.

The Prescient One, despite wearing the simple uniform of an elder instead of his signature teal cape and prosthetic makeup, had been recognized instantly. He could not walk freely through the Mall of Absolution as planned.

He whispered to one of the four bodyguards who were discreetly escorting him. Now that the ruse had failed, they would need to fall into standard protective formation.

And send one of the men ahead as a scout.

The Prescient One and his cohort soon arrived at a bakery that was renowned for its innovative methods. He was most interested in learning their secrets—and from one staff member in particular.

The advance scout greeted the group with a solemn nod, and the Prescient One gave his shoulder a friendly squeeze before entering the shop.

A vibrant birthday-style banner above the counter said, "Welcome to A Modest Celebration!" There were many colorful pastries in the glass display cases, as well as a selection of ornate cakes that awaited personalization.

The seating area had space for thirty, and the ten or so customers present turned away from their coffee and conversation when they realized who had just entered the shop.

"Welcome, Your Modness!"

The Prescient One looked up from the food offerings. A fifty-something woman wearing matching teal apron and chef's hat was smiling at him.

"Please," he said, motioning to his humble garb, "today you may refer to me as Elder Cullen."

"Certainly, Elder. Has something here caught your eye?" she added with a wink.

"Your culinary artistry is the talk of the Mall. I've come to be enlightened, and perhaps have a taste."

"In that case, we *must* give you a private tour of our kitchen. Please…"

The woman stepped to her right and pulled a door open. The Prescient One and a single guard passed through and followed her into the back of the bakery.

He saw several women working alone in brightly lit cubicles. Each was bent over a stone surface, carefully sculpting mounds of dough into different shapes and sizes.

The group stopped beside a young baker who was stuffing the contoured edges of a three-pronged metal frame.

"Eldress Foster," the clerk said, "a customer has expressed keen interest in how we create our leavened magic. Would you be so kind as to give a demonstration?"

"I'd be happy to." The woman set down her materials and looked up for the first time. "Who—"

There was a moment of silence as her eyes met those of the Prescient One. Neither broke contact for several seconds.

"Well," the clerk said, "I mustn't neglect the counter. I'll leave you to it." She scurried back toward the front of the shop, and the guard moved into a quiet corner of the kitchen.

"Hello, Julia," the Prescient One said.

The young baker blushed, then brought her powdery hands together. "Forgive me, Your Prescience. I almost didn't recognize you. But what is your reason for… dressing down?"

"So that you might call me by my real name. Scott."

"Did you… Do you really want to see what we do here?"

"Oh, yes. People say that your cakes are true works of art. As temporary as ice sculptures, but an altogether more interactive experience."

"Then come closer and I'll let you play appren— *novitiate* for a while." She smiled.

The cake was halfway finished and in the style of a medieval castle. Two perpendicular walls were held into form by interlocked baking sheets. Julia demonstrated how she filled the interior, layer by layer, with elements such as knights and thrones and tapestries using dyed dough and colorful candies.

Once the structure was complete, she sealed the outer walls and pressed two more baking sheets against them. Scott noticed that the bottom edges of these sheets also had metal roller wheels built within tiny coverings. When he inquired about this feature, Julia said, "That's to account for expansion while in the oven. The same goes for these small openings on top.

When the castle itself is done, I'll add the turrets and center spire which bake separately inside smaller molds. Then I'll apply the frosting and use this tool to create a realistic stone texture."

She picked up a flat metal square and pointed to the grooves and indents which covered one side. As Scott reached to inspect it, their fingers briefly touched.

He said, "I've thought about this moment a great deal. How I would thank you properly."

"Thank *me?* For what? I only had the honor of speaking to Your Prescience for a brief moment, back…"

"I remember our first meeting very well."

"But we barely exchanged more than a few pleasantries after the ceremony. You were so busy, understandably. How could I have… ?"

"Julia," Scott said quietly, "I was subjected to terrible psychological tortures while in captivity. I was forced to confront my oldest demons and my worst faults, until my entire being nearly fell away. Somehow I survived intact, and at first wondered if I had unlocked a new source of inner strength. But later, when my mind had truly cleared, I realized that there had been a guardian angel hovering over me. Her light guided me forward to make it through. Julia, it was the image of *your* smiling face on the day you advanced from lay member to eldress. It offered me *hope* for a wonderful future—if I could just hold on. And so I did. Now I can finally thank you. And perhaps one day, offer you more."

Eldress Julia Foster looked down. She brushed away some dried flakes from her apron, then shook her head slowly with compressed lips.

"I've thought about you too," she said at last. "But I had no reason to dream. There are hundreds of other women here at the Mall. And when you were gone, I cried—not knowing if they were the tears of a Modestian, or for myself."

"Julia, why *did* you join the Church?"

She smiled and turned away. "One step at a time, Mr. Cullen. But right now this cake is ready for the walk-in cooler. I do hope you've enjoyed the tour. Perhaps you'll come visit us again?"

After Julia had transferred the castle onto a rolling cart and began moving away, Scott placed the metal texture tool back onto her work table. The corner of a silver envelope peeked out from underneath.

"Indeed," he said. "Good day."

34. JUST GETTING STARTED

"But I'll tell you, that's why I pinched my nose and voted for Dominguez." The comic on stage shook his head. "At least a new president means you get to write fresh material. I swear, if I hear *one more* bit about crouching tigers, I'm gonna go to the zoo myself and throw Molotov cocktails at any cat I see!"

He snatched a beer bottle off the stool beside him and drank.

"Look, I've been in this comedy racket for over twenty years. Weathered all the storms, from political correctness to the anally retentive conservative types. And at the end of the day, I've always found a way to give politicians… a good roasting in effigy."

He grinned, cocking an eyebrow while adjusting his rimless spectacles.

"I can't seem to get a rise out of this MARVIN fellow, though. He won't take the bait! And so damn *honest*, my gosh, he won't even up your Debit Score for messing with him! Heh, good old MARVIN… But still, he scares me. I really think they opened up

Panderer's Box this time. Seems like every hour, another old evil deed shoots out like a firecracker! And then the world goes chasing after it like a bride's bouquet, because *there's gold in them debts!*

"I'll tell ya, know what we need right now? A real-life Ghostbusters squad! Suit 'em up and send 'em out into the streets. It's time to lock those ghosts *up!* And I, being so very handsome, would of course be perfect to cast as one of the male leads..."

Clyde Jenkins laughed along with the other audience members here at the Chuckle Condo on Sunset Boulevard. He glanced at the girl sitting beside him at this tiny round table near the stage. The lights reflected prettily against her eyes and cheeks.

Ekaterina Something. Ukrainian former figure skater now trying to make it big as an online fitness instructor. Three comics in and she had barely cracked a smile. Clyde wasn't even sure she remembered he was here.

But she was damn cute. Shoulder-length blond hair parted down the middle. Sharp pointed nose. Glitter sparkling on her eyelids. And a body toned to perfection from twirling on the ice her whole life.

Eddie had set them up to help Clyde get his mind off of Ayana. Expand his horizons by spending time with a white chick who wasn't from America. But Ekaterina had barely spoken the whole time, even during the car ride over from the lounge where they'd first met up. He'd tried to make small talk, but she mostly gave simple one- or two-word answers to his questions about her work and life back home.

Still, it was good to be out and about rather than back at his place pining for Ayana. Apparently she had flown out to whatever state they filmed her TV show in. Clyde didn't ask where—he didn't want to risk being seen as a stalker type anyway.

He heard Ekaterina laugh. That was a good sign. He glanced at her again, only to see that she was looking at her phone. She tapped around the screen, nodding and smiling at whatever was going on there.

Oh well...

"...you please give it up for a very good friend of mine, the star of *Shaquan's Razor*, the hilarious Mr. Freddie Overton!"

The host stepped back from the microphone stand with his arms raised triumphantly as a heavyset black man wearing a leather driving cap arrived on stage. The two men embraced, then the MC trotted away.

"Thank you, thank you," the comic said after pulling the mic free. "My goodness! Jason, that was such a touching introduction... So how y'all doin' tonight? I see a lot of lovely faces in the crowd, yes I do. How many of y'all ever had your nose broke? And I ain't talkin' about you girls who done got a little plastic surgery, you know, thinkin' it was your ticket to success in *this* town. Nah, I'm talking about like, in a fist fight."

Overton scanned the crowd for a moment.

"No? Guess we got some softies in attendance. Bunch of male models. Whateva. That's okay. But me? I'm from the *streets!* Had my nose broke twice in one *day!* That's right. From two pm until seven-fiddy, it was tilted *this* way. Then some cat named Trucka popped me, and my nose swung like the rudder of a damn boat back the other way.

"Oh my God. The blood was pourin' down my face. Trucka was flexin', askin' if I wanted any more. I told him, 'Attention, shipmates. This is your captain speaking. We're now heading in an easterly direction to get away from those dark, muscular clouds...' "

Clyde rolled in his seat along with the other people nearby as Freddie puttered around the stage while flipping his free hand back and forth above his nose. Because Clyde knew all about those days when trouble seemed to find a person from dawn to dusk. He'd never actually had his nose broken, but survived plenty of scraps all the same.

He took another peek at Ekaterina. She was staring blankly at the stage. Freddie's story had made zero impact upon her.

'Whateva' is right.

After a month of Hollywood fakery, it was refreshing to get a raw taste from this guy up on the stage. Clyde settled back into his seat, ready to absorb the rest of the act.

And who knew, maybe he'd ask the club manager if he could meet Freddie later on. DJ Clydoscope had millions of streams to his credit. Surely this comedian had heard his song once or twice…

"Okay, I go," Ekaterina said, yanking Clyde out of his reverie. He watched her zip a small handbag closed and then reach back to pull her jacket off the seat.

Stunned, all he could muster was, "Really? Now?"

"Sorry. Friends have something happening too."

She offered a halfhearted smile and stood up.

The comic saw Ekaterina put on her jacket and called after her, "Where you goin', girl? I'm just getting started up here." He winked. "But with *those* legs, I bet her night's just getting started too."

The audience whistled and jeered as Freddie simulated a sexy walk across the stage. Then the man dipped his head in Clyde's direction.

"Sorry, brutha man. Happens to us all. Now, where was I at? Oh yeah. Taking relationships to the 'let's move in together' phase. Note to you young fellas— *don't do it!* Trust me, because…"

Clyde sank further down in his seat and folded his arms. Another night ruined because of a girl. Another ego bruise because he'd signed up to be a little fish in a big pond.

Hmm. Guess I gotta flip my own rudder, head in another direction too.

35. EMERGENCY BROADCAST

"This is the Reverend Matthias G. Witherspoon of Akron, Ohio. I am coming to you live from an undisclosed location with an emergency broadcast.

"I regret to inform you, my loyal followers across the nation and around the world, that I have been driven out of my church. That's right, ladies and gentlemen, you heard correctly. Abandoned, denied, and unceremoniously removed from the property like a criminal.

"Psalm 41: 'Even my close friend, whom I trusted, who shared my bread, he has lifted up his heel against me.'

"I didn't know how long I would still have access to this PerformTube channel, so it was essential that I shared my side of the story before anyone else bore false witness and tarnished my good name.

"What happened? Why was I besieged there within my private chambers? The answer is as simple as it is tragic. No one wants to hear the truth. They're too proud to handle correction. But I won't stop, because I see that this country is *sinking*. So I got to speak up, no matter how costly it might prove for myself, a loyal servant of God.

"I declare that it is folly to blame political, economic, or cultural changes for our woes, because stacked on top of all that, we also got a weakness of spirit inside ourselves. Afflicting us from coast to coast, and in every pigment across the color spectrum. We are losing ourselves. And worst of all, we don't have the gumption to admit it.

"It seems to me that after millennia, humanity is *still* grappling with the same tired issues that destroyed so many civilizations of the past, before burying them under the dust. Hear me now, my people. When disagreement devolves into conflict, it can quickly spiral into violence. Today I walk away from my betrayers, whom I still love, to spare us from such awful consequences. It is most certainly better that we should all live and walk free. Better to carry the pain in our hearts for ugly words spoken, rather than regret actions which cannot be undone.

"Although my tenure at the Ministry of the Divine God appears to have concluded, know that Matthias G. *has not* lost his fighting spirit. And I will draw inspiration from the Lord Jesus Christ Himself by remembering that sometimes... it takes only one.

"As long as one man carries the flame of truth, God will prevail. I make this pledge to you courageous souls listening now. If it has been fated for me to abandon the city and roam the land as a nomad or bedraggled vagabond, just as so many saints and apostles and martyrs have done through the centuries, then so be it. Let all others bear the consequences for averting their eyes out of fear or expediency.

"Yes indeed, if the truth lives on in one man's heart, then surely we can rebuild anew once again. So stay strong, my fellow lovers of the gospel. I guarantee you that the lie cannot last forever. Why? Because it does not create, but only feeds upon the stores of bounty accumulated by the humble.

For those of you who still believe two plus two equals four, don't be afraid to walk out that door. 'Cause it's the deceivers that need *you!* They'll whisper into your ear and say that you should keep 'em around to remind you of how great you are. Don't fall for it! Don't believe it, not for one second! Resist that temptation, or your vanity shall fall prey to the locust lie.

"Old Matthias will now take the lead, so watch out! White flight ain't got *nothin'* on me! I too will abandon the city if that is my cross to bear. I just pray that I will find the strength to accept it with as much serenity as my Lord Jesus Christ. That I will walk His path with the same patient resignation as He did after being forsaken.

"Remember and remember again, that in dark times all a man need do is seek the truth. Protect it and speak it. Then, even if he is a wanderer for years and years, righteousness shall survive while the tallest of castles crumble.

"Romans 5: 'And not only this, but we also exult in our tribulations, knowing that tribulation brings about perseverance; and perseverance, proven character; and proven character, hope.'

"So persevere, we must! I will talk to you again soon, somehow and somewhere as I venture into the unknown. Fall from grace? Never! I *got* the grace! And like my Lord Jesus, I shall rise up and return, stronger than ever before. There is so much hot air left in these preachin' pipes, ladies and gentlemen, you have no idea. Do not worry about me. Instead, praise the Christian God, amen!

"This is your friend, the demoted but not demoralized Reverend Matthias G. Witherspoon, signing off from this outcast broadcast. God bless you, me, and these Disintegrating States of America."

36. THE QUEENMAKERS

"Did you know that Robinson Crusoe's island was a meritocracy?"

These were the first words spoken by a man whom Eileen Jeffries-Lao had never before met, on the night of a fundraising gala in Orange County many years ago. Eileen, who at the time was mother to a young daughter and also served on the local school board, did not know what to make of this odd introduction.

She had smiled respectfully and waited for the man to explain himself. Afterward, her life was never the same.

"But the problem is," he continued, "there's no glory or gold medals to be had when all your efforts are spent on mere survival."

"I take it you're not a fan of the novel?" Eileen had offered.

The man laughed, clinking glasses with her as he said, "No. But I am a fan of *you*."

Again speechless, Eileen glanced around the room while fiddling with her bracelet.

"Well, not just myself. Mrs. Jeffries-Lao, considering what you've achieved locally in only a few years, clearly you have a great career ahead of yourself."

"I thank you," she said. "And do hope you're right."

"So let me ask you this. Would you rather be queen of a small island, or perhaps someplace a bit more noteworthy?"

"I must say, Mr… ?"

"Kent."

"Mr. Kent, you flatter me, and I'm intrigued by your riddles. So please, do tell!"

He winked. "The sky's the limit, if you have the right team on your side."

"Ah," Eileen said warmly, at last understanding the point behind his Robinson Crusoe allusion. "But surely you believe that an educated modern woman can rise through the ranks on her own?"

They had both laughed at this, with Kent adding, "I never said I didn't. But consider an alliance with the people I represent as the express shuttle. And *you* have already earned a ticket on board…"

It had all been so friendly. Lively and complimentary banter right out in the open among the other notable members of Orange County politics. And the gregarious Mr. Kent had most certainly delivered on his promises.

Eileen Jeffries-Lao next served a brief term as a California state representative, before vaulting into the governor's mansion. And then, in the blink of an eye, she was President of the United States—and in fact, could not have done it without his organization's influence.

A younger, more naive version of herself would have added "not so quickly" as a qualifier, but the fatigued and battle-tested Eileen of 2029 knew better.

Because the club which had extended her a membership believed in a world ordered by more than *merit* alone.

Networks. Alliances. Fifty-year plans. Blackmail and the promise of mutually assured incrimination. Fail-safes put in place to promote or clip the wings of ambitious individuals. Tools used to maintain global security—or orchestrate chaos.

Eileen Jeffries-Lao almost pitied the people who worried that the HRA's centralized supercomputer might usher in a surveillance state. The headless system had already been compiling dossiers on any and all potential *Who's Who* candidates for decades.

She herself had fallen into their trap long before ever appearing on their radar, however. As the daughter of exiles from Communist China, she understood perfectly why the government might keep tabs on any of her youthful political involvements. But no, she'd been ensnared far differently, and to this day still shook her head in disgusted admiration of their methods.

They had evidence of one of her few lifetime indiscretions filed away within their stockpiles of blackmail, like some grotesque variation of a De Beers warehouse, which stored human foibles instead of diamonds. A drunken romantic tryst after a night of letting loose with college friends. Sex in the bushes outside of a small hotel where some backpackers from Holland were staying.

Through all of human history, the worst that such liaisons produced was an unplanned pregnancy. And prior to the internet era, perhaps this scene would have gone no further than becoming part of some pervert's celluloid collection, with the sole copy eventually gathering dust in a cluttered attic.

But in the twenty-first century, that security camera

footage was used to control a woman long before she ever became the leader of the free world—and today it continued to steer her administration's agenda.

Eileen in her darkest moments fantasized about one day revealing all on a hot mic. In a flash, the general public would be thrust into an existential crisis about how their world actually operated. But besides putting her family in mortal danger, such a confession was not in keeping with her temperament—a metric which surely had been scrutinized before she was tapped to join the group that owned her.

Eileen Jeffries-Lao would never disclose their secrets willingly. Because she had been able to reach levels of success that far surpassed her Asian family's towering expectations. Because she had gotten to live the good life, never soiling her hands with peasant labor, while also making a positive impact for the working people of her adopted country.

And ultimately she believed—or had been convinced—that the masses needed to be led. A billion Robinson Crusoes, however competent, would only result in more inefficiency and disorder. But with the proper guiding hand, humanity might be capable of the kind of cooperation needed to conquer deep space.

This ethereal, majestic vision brought her to a state of calm that was as genuine as it was elusive. Glorious spaceships lifting off to leave all of the cruelty and filth and betrayal behind. The human race proclaiming to the universe that it had finally overcome its built-in flaws, which seemed to express themselves in a million destructive ways each day.

On the eve of her second inauguration, Eileen Jeffries-Lao took solace in the thought that, despite her own failings and regrets, she was helping to set the stage for the species' next great act.

37. GRAND PLOT

It was like old times again. Chris, Glenn, and Kate were hanging out and shooting the breeze. Cold beers for the guys and Kate was drinking hot tea.

"Cheers," Chris said, "to the rest of our lives."

"Cheers!" the others replied and beverages were clinked.

"So Glenn," Kate said, "what's the theme of your next song gonna be? Pro- or anti-government?"

Glenn gave a mild laugh. "You can guess what I was thinking while I was stuck in solitary. But now that I'm out… Think I'll just sit back and enjoy the taste of freedom for a while." He took a big gulp of beer.

"Not to rush you, but I've heard *somebody* practicing in his office a lot lately."

"Oh yeah?" Glenn thumped Chris on the arm. "Keepin' your chops up or writing some new riffs?"

Chris smiled bashfully. "I got a couple chord progressions I'm working on. Mapped out some drums too. But lyrics aren't my department, so…"

"Aha! This whole get-Glenn-out-of-jail thing has

been a grand plot to reunite the band. Well played, you two!"

They all laughed.

A moment later, Glenn added, "But seriously, thank you so much for everything. I could've been locked up for a long time. So maybe I do owe you at least one song, Chris."

"Hell yeah! We'll, uh, sing about international stuff so the Feds don't reconsider their decision to let you go."

"And what about the fate of your current band?" Kate asked.

"You know how it goes," Glenn replied. "Controversy equals notoriety. A lot more downloads. The other guys even had to reorder shirts from the printer twice! I figure we might be able to get on a decent tour as the opening act later in the spring. So you might even say, I fought the law… and I won!"

"Sell-out," Chris grinned.

"Heh, yeah. And Kate, you're back working local again?"

"The old grind," she said. "But things definitely seem different now. I'm not sure if it's all in my mind, or maybe the administration will just never feel as electric as it once did. And no, Glenn, I don't blame *you* for it."

Chris looked down, wary that this get-together had the potential to crash and burn at any second.

Glenn fiddled with his glass. "I will neither confirm nor deny anything that relates to the Jubileers. But I wanted to ask you, did the HRA foreign legion not float your boat or what?"

"Now it's my turn to be diplomatic," Kate said. "Let's just say, my own goals will be better achieved here on the mainland."

She reached out and scratched Chris on the back. He nodded, saying, "I'm glad you're here. Both of you. My two favorite people, ever."

"Come on, guys," Glenn said. "Enough with the weepy emo stuff. We're one year away from a new decade. What disasters can we clean up?"

"Oh god, here we go again," Kate said jokingly. "Anyone got a pen and paper handy for lyric ideas?"

"Always. Because a true artist never lets his guard down. Chris, you in?"

Chris rolled his eyes. "Duh! Why do you think we invited you out? To just have fun? Let's do this! Yup, the old gang's back at it. DIY fixes for top-heavy crises."

"Ooh," Kate marveled. "Looks like maybe we've got *two* wordsmiths here."

The trio laughed again, then got to work trying to solve all of the world's problems…

38. NO SIGN OF RECOGNITION

Clyde had been on his best behavior all day. Anywhere he was supposed to stand, or when asked to repeat a choreographed move fifteen times—he did it all professionally.

There were a lot of people running around this small warehouse soundstage, even though today was just a dry-run rehearsal in preparation for his upcoming video with DJ Low Bought. There was going to be CGI, and possibly real flames, so the production team wanted to capture some test footage to make sure the planned spectacle turned out larger than life.

A white girl with curly brown hair and a walkie-talkie on her hip approached.

"Hey, Clyde. The crew's all going on break, so we won't need you for a while. Feel free to grab a snack from craft services, and we'll find you in a bit."

She was on the move again before he'd even said "thanks."

Clyde ambled away from his spot in front of the green screen and went looking for the food tables. At one point, he passed several other crew members who were huddled around a gear cart deep in conversation.

After loading up his plate with some fruit and chips, Clyde wandered around the warehouse lazily while humming a tune. He almost stumbled over DJ Low, who was partially hidden within several black curtains that hung down from the rafters.

"Oh, Clyde," Low said from his electric scooter. "There you are. Good, good. Come on in and join me."

Clyde grabbed a plastic folding chair that was nearby and dragged it into the small enclosure. "What's the word, Low?" he asked.

The other rapper cleared his throat—he had a dry, raspy voice that made him sound much older than twenty-six.

"How you handlin' yourself?"

"Aw, you know. Tryin' to learn, day by day. It's the only way."

"Right, right. Well, look. I been watchin' you, and you know, you aight."

Clyde jabbed a finger at the food on his plate. "Thanks, man. You know, this whole thing kinda weird. Eddie told me the deal witchu back at the beginning, but still, I didn't know how to act around you."

Low rubbed his rough and wiry beard as he smiled. "Nah, you doin' fine. That's why I want to talk to you one on one. It's gonna be a huge deal, this reveal about my 'recovery.' We got to be on the same page when the firestorm hits."

"You think people gon' be mad when we tell 'em hard-cortex rap ain't for real?"

"No doubt. Because, that *is* the plan!" Low paused for a moment. "So I been running this LA hustle for a while now. Got a lot figured out. But you're new around here. I got to make sure you always land on your mark."

Clyde pointed his thumb in the direction of the set. "We been doin' that all morning, bro. I got it. I know where to step."

"Nah, kid. Forget about all that. I'm trying to take your head to another *level*."

"Oh… Like… ?"

"Like gettin' you to think about the dynamics of your surroundings. Look at all this right here. The building, the lights, the gear, all the people it take to run the show. It ain't cheap! And *we* are the main attraction."

"For real, though. But can't be nothin' wrong with that. Means we made it!"

Clyde offered a high-five, but Low waved it away with annoyance. The man said, "I keep asking myself why, of all types of art out there, why are they sinking their cash into hip-hop? And of all the things these folks on the crew could be doing with their time, with their skills… Why are they workin' with *me*, a hustla from the streets?"

"To make that money?" Clyde offered. "Or they just know what's hot."

Low scoffed. "Kid, our rhymes might be good, but they ain't *that* good. Like I said, there's another level I been chewin' on. So buckle up."

Clyde smiled and popped a grape into his mouth.

"All these white folks that move to LA, they don't just come here looking *for* something. I think they also tryin' to get *away* from something. But it ain't even that, 'cause the word that keeps coming into my mind is 'renunciation'. They are *renouncing* something about their white-bread Midwest world, and LA is the temple where they make the blood sacrifice to get their revenge."

"Whoa. Um… and how do we fit in? They gonna sacrifice *us*?"

"No, Clyde. Worse. They *romanticize* us."

"Huh? No way, hold up." Clyde sat forward and said, "I got to disagree on that. 'Cause I remember firsthand *those* types of Caucs from back in the day, when the HRA got started. They all came to the hood stupid as, patted us on the head, nothin' worked, and then after a while they was gone."

DJ Low Bought closed his eyes for a moment, then said, "You ain't totally wrong, but... Okay. This crew on set here, they all *competent*. They're the opposite of what you was just talkin' about. They know what they doin' and *still* they hoverin' around us. So if they ain't dumb, and they qualified to work on movies or the opera or whatever, why in the hell they wanna be with rappers instead of their own kind?!"

Clyde said, "Maybe 'cause they're colorblind? Equal opportunity and such?"

Low tapped his temples with his fingertips. Finally he said, "People in the know say I pulled this lobotomy stunt to stick it to white people for patronizing us. But truth is, I decided to hunker down because I needed time to think."

"So now, if you 'bout ready to come out of your stupor, that mean you got your solution?"

"Eh... I got a bit more understanding. I just don't know if it's the answer I wanted. Clyde, tell me, you know what a mandarin is?"

"Mandarin chicken? Oh yeah! Yum!"

"No, you fool! I'm talkin' 'bout mandarin Caucs!"

"Huh? Saaaaay what?"

Low leaned in very close, speaking quietly but with a harsh intensity. "It come from China. All the little bureaucratic types who waddle around messin' with everybody's business. They got no balls, but still think *they* should be the king. They smart, but they stupid. *However*, on the flip side—they also stupid, but smart. Chew on that riddle!"

Clyde stared blankly in confusion. "DJ, I…"

"All these Caucs in here are too afraid to step in front of that camera themselves and show they face to the world. But they still hold all the levers of power. Location, materials, funding…"

"But I got money now too—"

"Shut yo' mouth, boy! I'm layin' down some truth. Without them and their whole setup, we'd all just be rappin' on the stoop, hoping to catch a few quarters while dodging bullets from some other brother's pistol. So why is it that you and I are here at this goddamn warehouse, when there's a thousand dudes who can play Mozart on the cello that ain't nobody gonna see in no video?"

"I don't *know*, Low, so tell me!"

"Because all these Caucs are *sick!* Sick in they soul. So sick, they'll use their hard-earned skills to film me drooling, rather than true art, because something inside them says they need to cater to us Minoricans. Yup, yup, we're their little babies! Got to coddle us and push us down the street in a stroller!"

Just then, one of the crew members poked his head through the curtains.

"Hey, fellas! The director's back on set and ready to start blocking out the next sequence of moves. As soon as you can, we'd love to see you out there."

"Aight, cool," Clyde said. He turned to DJ Low Bought and added, "Chat's over for now, I gue—"

He did a double-take.

The other man had slumped forward in his scooter. A long stalactite of spittle dangled above his kneecap as he whimpered in a falsetto, "Ma-ma… Da-da… Ma-ma…"

Clyde looked into the DJ's eyes, but there was no sign of recognition. He got up shakily and left his plate on the folding chair, then followed the PA toward set.

His mind was in a daze.

39. OBSESSED WITH RACE

Rebellican Senator Victor Dominguez was neither grateful nor bitter as he arrived outside the Capitol Building for the inauguration ceremony of Eileen Jeffries-Lao. Slightly grumpy perhaps, but no one who had ever lost an election felt particularly well on the day that their opponent was sworn into office.

It could have been worse. As a consequence of his Debit Score lurching skyward after he appeared on *DDM TV Live* back in early December, he might have been assigned to a lengthy term at some community service project doing God-knows-what.

But Jeffries-Lao had deemed his patriotic takedown of the conspiracy-minded Cornelius Alemán sufficient grounds for canceling out whatever DDM punishment was due. The aging scion Alemán remained one of the few players involved in the recent political scandals whose charges had not been dropped. The man did, however, tap into his wealthy network of allies to acquire the ten million dollars necessary to post bail, and then promptly fled to South America. His whereabouts were currently unknown.

Victor himself was now free to return to the Senate and serve out the final two years of his term. Whether he would run for re-election was debatable. On the one hand, he knew Eileen Jeffries-Lao so well that he could act as a formidable watchdog. However, the presidential election campaign had taken so much out of Victor that he didn't think he had another go in him —especially not when his three children back home in Flagstaff needed his guidance.

As he took his seat in the gallery next to his wife Jaclyn, Victor quietly resolved that he would only stay in Washington for the next two years. But each day, working to put the pieces in place so that the president found herself in check at every turn.

Why? Because the percentage of the population that had voted for Victor was much larger than expected. Because he believed that the damage done in a Dramacrat president's second term was always magnitudes worse than during the first. And because, despite his own proclamations on *DDM TV* that Eileen Jeffries-Lao was a dutiful American, Victor sensed that her demeanor had subtly changed in the weeks following the Holy Holidays. Was it just relief after two election-season scares—or was something more sinister lurking behind her piercing eyes?

Victor drifted off into his own thoughts amid the drawn-out pomp and circumstance of the ceremony. But something Jeffries-Lao said must have rattled his subconscious, because suddenly he found himself paying careful attention to her words.

"...time marches on, history places new challenges before us, and we must meet them directly. If we cannot afford to perpetually relive the past, then we must also not allow ourselves to fixate on the present moment.

"My first term could be defined as having led a united national effort to restore a sense of fairness. In my second term, we will use this repaired root system to launch ourselves farther than we have ever gone before.

"For decades, First World nations have tried to feed and clothe the poorest of countries. But how many containers full of grain and second-hand fashions can we send, before needing to find a new higher goal? One that will tap into and inspire the global community, which has become so interconnected via the power of the internet this century?

"I say that goal will be to fulfill the dream presently incubating in places like the research laboratories of Palo Alto, California... the test launch sites at Cape Canaveral, Florida... as well as in the heart of every child who aspires to be an astronaut.

"You know, some of the critics have said that my administration is obsessed with race. To them I say, you're right! And just you watch how determined we will be to achieve great things in this next phase of the *space* race! Where by working together, governments all around the world will ensure that soon, very soon, human colonies on Mars and the Moon are not simply Hollywood productions on the silver screen."

"Jesus Christ," Victor heard someone mutter. "It's JFK all over again."

"...one such priority," Eileen continued, "is to avoid the stagnation that comes from trying to reinvent the wheel over and over again. Especially now, when there are multistage rockets waiting to be built..."

Victor Dominguez got a chill in his bones. He sensed that something fanatical was bleeding through the president's normally unflappable veneer. Passion for scientific endeavors was of course commendable, but he found what Jeffries-Lao exuded from the podium today greatly unnerving.

He would indeed keep a close eye on her during the coming months. Because if her plans continued to diverge so far from what she had campaigned on, then how many economic sectors—or Americans in general—might be left behind in her zeal to open up the far reaches of space?

Victor Dominguez vowed to make the President of the United States work for every step. The nation could always recover from a stumble, but perhaps not after leaping off whatever cliff Eileen Jeffries-Lao was fixated upon.

40. THE DEVIL YOU KNOW

The Prescient One leaned in very close and said, "Have you ever faced two intertwined choices that were so potentially volatile, you couldn't even think clearly?"

He heard the proponent on the other side of the partitioned booth clear his throat. Then the man said, "Are you able to offer any specifics? I understand that people often visit a direction booth due to the sensitive nature of their concerns. However, if I am to help steer you effectively, it would be better to share as many details as you can."

"I see." The Prescient One took a slow breath. "One path involves oaths and legalities. The consequences of breaking these would be quite detrimental to me. Not only that, but speaking up will also bring disturbing new truths to light. Perhaps this is necessary."

"My heavens! And your *second* dilemma?"

"It regards my potential happiness. I know that her heart is there for the taking."

"Oh, yes?" the proponent said, his voice fluttering. "So what about these seemingly distinct issues gives you pause?"

"If I expose the first, no one will be able to control the fallout from the scandal. I would also be severely punished—meaning that she and I could not be together."

The Prescient One heard the bench creak as the proponent leaned away from the mesh screen that separated their faces. His own face was bare, having made the decision to stop applying prosthetic makeup altogether after first presenting himself to Julia in the flesh.

The other man said, "You are a brave Modestian for entrusting your hopes and fears with me, a mere believer. It seems as if you have come to one of the defining crossroads of your life. So we must ask, where do a person's obligations to society end? When are they worth the ultimate sacrifice? But consider, no one should be a slave to the masses—you too deserve all the happiness that such altruism ensures for others."

"Perhaps I have been addicted to sacrifice. The promise to myself always being of course, that *this* selfless act will be the last."

"Oh, but it is!" the proponent said. "Until the next, and the next after that."

The Prescient One nodded his head slowly. "Ah. Good men and women have many opportunities to prove their charitable nature. But the moments which might change their own lives are quite rare."

"Yes, exactly! And if a self-interested act results in a person's heart overflowing, then their capacity to give is also replenished for years to come. Conversely, neglecting our human needs can sap us of the strength to be our best."

"Then the second matter is settled. I will ask her hand in marriage."

"Wonderful!"

"But still, the first… It cannot be ignored."

The proponent lowered his voice. He said, "What would be the worst-case outcome if you remained silent?"

"The devil you know." The Prescient One rose. "Thank you so very much for helping me work through these troubling questions. Mod be with you."

"And also with you…"

A short while later, the Prescient One was standing in his private study. Laid out on the desk before him were a white sheet of paper and a small zip-seal plastic bag which contained a soiled napkin. Printed on the page were the lab results of a sample taken from this napkin.

He recalled the words of the technician who had discussed the shocking implications with him earlier in the day.

"Something is distorting her DNA sequence."

"But for how many years?" the Prescient One had responded. "Surely an old item stolen from her home in California by an enterprising thief would match what we have?"

The tech shook his head in confusion. "I'm just a data guy, Your Prescience. I would assume you know more about the world of politicians than I do."

"Wait… Are you saying she may have been… obscuring… or scrambling… her DNA for years? Before MARVIN was even an idea?"

"It's possible."

"But how…" The Prescient One trailed off. "How could it happen that I got such a pure sample?"

The technician's jaw clenched. He said, "Either she takes regular doses, like a prescription, or normally no one is able to get their hands on her saliva like you did."

"So… She pops a pill or receives an injection each morning? Or anytime she's about to interact with the public? Maybe that's it! She only needs to be careful when she's exposed. Her handlers must also do some sort of cleanup afterward."

"And with you incarcerated at the time, she didn't think she had anything to worry about."

The Prescient One now looked down at the sealed napkin and lab printout. Two seemingly innocuous items, which together had the power to turn the world upside down.

Because if Victor Dominguez deserved to be raked over the coals of ancestral shame for the crimes of a mid-nineteenth-century Mexican *bandito*, then what might be the fitting punishment if Eileen Jeffries-Lao's unadulterated genetic history came to light?

The Prescient One closed his eyes and pictured a montage of Chinese peasants and warriors falling down dead through the centuries. Eileen's own distant relatives had long-forgotten blood on their hands—but the body count paled in comparison to anything that Chairman Mao had achieved during a single year of his twentieth-century reign.

Next he imagined the tumultuous scenes that might play out after the president's revised Debit Score was announced. Calls for her resignation. Political defenders and opponents at each other's throats. Was *this* inconvenient archive radioactive enough to break America's long chain of peaceful transitions of power… or even usher in a second civil war?

For him to remain silent—to sacrifice the truth in the name of stability—would be perhaps as strategic as it was prudent. Because now the Prescient One was armed with something no one else had: proof that for many years, a hidden network had groomed Eileen Jeffries-

Lao. First for her role as president, and then to serve as the global ambassador promoting interplanetary exploration.

In secrecy, he would remain free to keep watchful eye from his position of chastened church leader. To map out the organization's structure. Gather information about its members. Undermine their conspiratorial plans...

And he would have the strength to keep fighting for what was right in a world being poisoned by snakes that slithered in the shadows. Because he had finally reached that place of joy which he sought for so long in the trenches of blind grueling effort. Soon, Julia Foster would be his bride.

The Prescient One locked the damning pieces of evidence inside a hidden wall safe. There they would remain, he hoped for all time.

He took a private elevator to his sleeping quarters for a brief rest. Afterward, he would still his fluttering heart and call upon the woman whose memory had given him the will to survive weeks of torture—and all the while, keeping an incriminating napkin hidden from his jailers.

41. FOR THE CHILDREN

Nolan Simmons closed up the gear supply closet, then looked in on the roomful of young computer techs while heading to the elevator. There they all were in near-darkness, tapping away at their workstations and completely focused on the task at hand. They were so sharp, so intuitive, so effective.

These were the brightest of the street kids that Nolan had plucked out of the bedlam and trained in electronics. The public schools had been of no use to them—how many were once habitually truant students, but now eagerly showed up here three days a week?

An unconventional setup to say the least, but it wasn't Nolan's fault that yet another government body which functioned on the surface—the buses ran their routes and the teachers' unions got funded—still let entire generations of poor kids slip through the cracks.

Stepping away from the computer lab, Nolan thought about the powder keg of archival information that these geniuses were dredging up. In truth, he was implicating them as accomplices in what might be considered a threat to national, if not global security. The boys, meanwhile, thought it was great fun to see who among them could gather the most historical data. The rankings posted on a whiteboard in glowing neon ink were updated at the end of each week.

As he arrived back at the custom-built video editing room, Nolan wondered if he really ought to just be grateful for the financial windfall that producing Clyde's first music video had blessed him with. Meaning that he would need to cancel this "Great Library of Newark" project, and instead let whoever was in charge of worldwide Reparations roll it out on their own schedule.

Nolan felt like he was caught in a vise. Simply *possessing* this information was so risky. An FBI raid was quite possible, even if none of the tech kids mistakenly leaked any of it. And what would *that* scene look like? A bunch of eight- to eleven-year-olds working in violation of child labor laws, now being led away in handcuffs!

Everything that Nolan had worked for would crumble after that. He would never make good on his silent promise to the neighborhood. No, he could not put that at risk...

But even if he scrubbed every last bit of data from his network, a savvy government cybersecurity expert could probably trace its route through the public fiber-optic pipes. If Nolan instead threw caution to the wind and opened the spigots, the fallout would likely be so chaotic that no one would have time to pursue the source for weeks or months. And at that point, perhaps society would consider the deed as having been a public service.

Because Nolan was of the belief that secretly filling up a reservoir with obfuscations and lies, while also grandstanding about the audit being conducted overseas—it could only lead to an even more disastrous reckoning than whatever he had the power to provoke now.

While he wasn't as qualified as a lawyer or politician to weigh all the merits of the situation, Nolan simply could not allow *more* chains to be wrapped around humanity's psyche. And here he agreed with that masked Sentinels of Jubilee speaker, who during the original hack had warned against the dangers of arbitrarily bottling up creative potential in the name of short-term punitive thinking.

Having seen his platoon of tech geeks in action only moments ago, Nolan truly understood how tremendous the possibilities were. Somehow he would have to find the courage to unleash the digital deluge—for the sake of future generations and the unimaginable greatness they would surely achieve...

But an hour later, as he sat nursing a glass of whiskey, Nolan Simmons still couldn't believe that he was the one who had been fated to launch this supernova of a truth bomb on the unsuspecting world. No military man, despite his training, could truly predict what he would do in moments fraught with so much responsibility.

"At least those guys have their orders," Nolan said to himself quietly.

A stream of catch phrases suddenly popped into his head.

Just do it.

Do the right thing.

If it feels good, do it.

Do what you gotta do.

He held the tumbler under his nose, and sweet warm tones emanated into his nostrils. He would have to decide sooner rather than later. Because in less than two weeks, Black *History* Month would begin.

Nolan thought of his young apprentices once again, and another cliche came to mind. It was perhaps the most overused justification for any and all policies, pleas, and interventions over the past fifty years.

Do it for the children.

Nolan Simmons took a sip of whiskey and closed his eyes with a wary smile.

Because he just might have to.

42. INAUGURAL BALL

"So, Mr. Richards, I hear you're thinking of leaving us."

Ryan Richards flashed one of his trademark million-dollar smiles and guided his dance partner along with the flow of the room. A nineteenth-century waltz filled the air.

"That *is* a possibility," he said vaguely.

He felt a hard squeeze on the shoulder before Eileen Jeffries-Lao leaned in close and breathed into his ear, "Just tell me what you need, Ryan. More money? An hour-long puff piece about your life? How about a star on the Walk of Fame?"

"Haha, that *would* be tempting."

"Or perhaps, as the ultimate proof that you had triumphed over your B-movie career, a night's stay in the Lincoln Bedroom?"

"Me, a guest at the White House?"

"Oh yes, certainly. Because… These last few years, using entertainment to help bolster cultural acceptance of Reparations… Your show has been instrumental in achieving that goal. And *you* have been an inspiration, sir."

"Well, Madam President, I'm flattered. Truly. And *DDM* has had a good run, but…"

"Look, buster. You threw your lot in with the HRA and have done quite well for yourself."

Richards tried to pull away. He said testily, "Yeah, I know. But all these changes to the show make me nervous. We've lost our edge. I'd rather not be there when the ratings tank."

"Don't worry," Eileen assured him with a light pat on the lapel of his tuxedo blazer. "We'll tell your agent when it's time to start auditioning for something new."

"I don't know…"

"Ryan, my administration always takes care of its loyal soldiers." Eileen got very close now. She said, "And so, during your visit, if you'd like for someone who's say, blond… around five-seven… to place a mint on your pillow… That can all be arranged."

"Madam Pres—"

"Ha, don't give me any of that, Ryan. I know all about your reputation. You might be able to blush for the TV cameras on cue, but I'd find that hard to believe in your private life."

Richards glanced around the room at the elegantly dressed dancers and other guests who were mingling at the edges. "We're all taking one for the team, eh? How long am I supposed to stay on?"

He felt her thumb dig into his hip bone as they entered a crush of bodies on the dance floor.

"Just one more year," the president said fervently. "We all have to hold on for another year."

"One thing, though. There aren't any hidden cameras inside Lincoln's old playpen, are there?"

"Not a chance. Guaranteed to be clean. We perform a

sweep before every guest's arrival. For *everyone's* sake."

"I see," Richards said breezily. "Guess I'll have to film Miss Five-Seven myself…"

"…then the world is ours."

Presidential Chief of Staff Tony Rizzuto had spoken these words to help soothe Eileen Jeffries-Lao's nerves the week before Tribesgiving. If they could just stay calm through the inauguration, he'd promised, then they would have four years to shape the future together.

Of the nation. Of the world. And their illicit relationship.

But now, with the oaths taken and festivities reaching a fever pitch, he found that his own anxieties were actually getting worse…

He was married to a beautiful woman who had given him two children. Alana Rizzuto could also be counted on to support his every career move—both vertically and across the country when duty called. He saw her standing near the cocktail bar, patiently listening to some blowhard from the State Department regale her with stories that were as unverifiable as they were self-aggrandizing.

How had he gotten himself romantically involved with a Chinese-American woman nearly ten years his senior? It all began during the chaos leading up to the election. That sudden fear of losing power had brought them so much closer—and now he was risking everything that truly mattered to him for… what, exactly?

What did he want with *the world*, if one day his son Doyle didn't respect him because he had been outed as the president's gigolo in some tabloid?

And if that potential shame wasn't reason enough for

Tony Rizzuto to seek a way out, he had also recently noticed some concerning quirks in his mistress's behavior. Bizarre declarations that were followed by a grating cackle. She'd even left a few classified documents which were far above his pay grade out in the open during one of their clandestine sleepovers.

The autumnal haze of tension, triumph, and lust was finally giving way to a sober clarity. Where did his loyalties ultimately lie? Could his career and personal obligations be reconciled? And which would take precedence, should they ever diverge?

Because if Eileen Jeffries-Lao was at risk of becoming a madwoman, then he himself might be more effective than anyone else at warding off disaster—which meant he would need to remain close by her side. Could he do that *and* end their affair? If he stayed on as chief of staff to protect her, surely he would also be expected to fill the role of male comforter, perhaps going through the motions for *years*...

Tony Rizzuto was revolted by such a prospect. He had been a varsity high school linebacker. Had graduated from Penn in three years before earning his master's degree at Georgetown University. Never could he have imagined that his legacy might be defined not by personal achievements, but as just another Beltway insider who couldn't keep it in his pants.

Or, he could simply walk away. Cite stress or some other health reason for taking a brief leave of absence. Then, having bought a little time before Eileen suspected anything was amiss, move his family out of their Bethesda home under the cover of night.

But where would he take them?

Any place that was safely out of range from the blast crater Eileen Jeffries-Lao might make of his life.

First Man Paul Jeffries had set a rule for himself: no more than one drink per hour when appearing in public. If he faltered, he was then obliged to speak to the ugliest or dullest person in his vicinity until back on schedule. Such was his burden on those important occasions when he absolutely must not bring embarrassment to all things presidential.

A quick glance into each of the venue's rooms confirmed that tonight his resolve would surely be put to the test—if only because there were so many beautiful ladies in attendance.

And Paul, in his more roguish moments, sought to model himself after the aristocratic dandy that Ben Franklin became when touring France later in life. He tried to ignore the whispers insinuating that his affairs with much younger women were not conquests, but in fact sad compensation after years of being emasculated throughout Eileen's political career.

It had once been said, that while everyone looked forward to the day when the United States of America elected its first female president, no one actually wanted to be that woman's husband. The singular distinction had befallen Paul Jeffries—and it would be his ultimate legacy when all the biographies were trimmed to mere paragraphs.

No one would ever remember the jazz power trio he had founded back in the early 1990s. Himself on guitar and backing vocals. Ronald Lewis pounding the drums. And fronted by the inimitable Monty Castillo, whose voice and fretless bass lines were silkier than ice cream on a hot summer day.

They were an interracial Bay Area staple back before anyone kept obsessive tabs about identity. Parrot Esoteric, as they were called, tapped into the freewheeling spirit of the sixties and seventies, when

creativity swirled in a glorious mishmash of styles—
then refined it with the technical proficiency and
production quality of the eighties. All that AOR rock
and the finger-tapping solos made famous by the hair
metal bands on MTV, inspired The Parrot to take their
own musical vision to the next level, rather than sit
back comfortably and rehash the past.

The national artistic scene was overflowing at this
time, with original hip-hop and alternative rock, as well
as thoughtful movies that captured everyone's different
experiences. But then something seemed to shift
imperceptibly almost overnight, and people scuttled
away from one another to retrench in a fog of
misunderstanding and isolation.

Was it grunge suddenly toppling the radio-rock
dynasties from the album charts? Michael Jordan's
shocking retirement from basketball after three straight
championships? Or Bill Clinton sliding into the Oval
Office because an upstart third-party candidate had
split the vote?

No matter what the true cause, everyone knew in
their hearts that the light and exuberant feeling of the
eighties had been irretrievably lost.

For the young Paul Jeffries, it meant that so-called
serious music quickly fell out of favor. Attendance
dropped at the gigs which became fewer and far
between. Soon Monty was spending more and more time
down in Miami playing in bands with his fellow Cubans.
And Ronald, who was always in demand, ended up
making a career out of touring with established groups
that were in need of a skilled drummer.

Which left a deflated Paul vulnerable to the *sensible*
appeals of his parents back in Upstate New York, who
offered to fund graduate school even if he insisted upon
staying out on the West Coast. He spent the rest of the
decade puttering around the campuses of Cal-Berkeley

and Stanford, compiling degrees in history and business management—while also futilely playing out on weekend nights hoping for the break that never came.

Then one evening late in 1999, he met a vital Asian-American woman who was a decade younger than himself. He saw in her eyes the kind of appreciation that had eluded him for years.

Paul thought it was he who had pursued her, and only much later realized that their courtship had been a strategic game on her part. Demure interest followed by hesitant acquiescence, and then total submission to his sexual desires—right up until the day he awoke to discover that the former Eileen Lao had not inspired him toward greatness, but in fact supplanted the last vestiges of his inner fire.

He eyed her now from across the ballroom. She was dancing too closely with some suntanned son of a bitch whose capped teeth glared in the chandelier light as he whispered into her ear.

Paul Jeffries found himself alternately enraged, humiliated, thirsty, and horny. He felt the urge to lose himself in a haze of cocktails while flirting with any number of the women in attendance for whom this event was a life highlight. He could take one of them to a hotel—or some supply closet here at the venue—and unleash all of his frustration out on her with animalistic fury, knowing that she would file the whole night's experience away as a thrilling secret memory.

But instead of allowing a petulant reaction to ruin his night—not *this* early, at least—Paul turned away and entered another space where a live band was up on stage. He ordered a vodka-soda from the bar and watched the blues-rock quintet play a few songs. After finishing his drink, he ascended the steps that led up to the stage platform.

He waved casually at the black bandleader until he

got the man's attention, then mimicked strumming a guitar. Paul had noticed that this guy was a solid player in his own right—a fellow also-ran who nobody ever heard of, fated to a lifetime of performing other musicians' hits at weddings and parties.

"Ladies and gentlemen," Paul heard the man say a few minutes later, "we have a surprise guest joining us on stage right now. Please put your hands together for the First Man himself, Mr. Paul Jeffries…"

He fell into the rhythm of a sixties classic, his neck oscillating slowly with the groove of a drumbeat that felt suspended in time. Paul took great satisfaction when, out of the corner of his eye, he saw the bandleader do a double-take after he bent and held a succulently sweet note high up on the third string. Because this wasn't pretend. Not some phony smile for the cameras, either. This was music from the soul. Making magic in real time. Touching people on a level beneath the skin—and far beyond what could be expressed with words.

In that wonderfully pure moment, on a night to celebrate his wife's grand triumph, First Man Paul Jeffries looked back on the last thirty years of his life with a bewildered sense of clarity. So much of it had been lost to waste and distraction and merely going through the motions—the drunkenness, the affairs, the thousand meaningless social functions he'd been forced to attend.

And despite it all, while commanding a stage he had imposed himself upon, Paul Jeffries showed the world that he could still summon God with a Fender Stratocaster and speak His Word in 4/4 time.

He closed his eyes, tapping his foot steadily as he let the tragic weight of all that could have been fall away, and wailed on a solo for the ages…

Eileen was mortified. Someone had pulled her aside to let her know that Paul was prancing around up on stage making a scene. She simply couldn't believe it. On this of all nights.

But there he was, sweating and making faces and leaning back to back with the bass player, each of them smiling and looking up to the heavens. The singer crooned, then threw his arm over Paul's shoulders as the old fool twiddled his fingers on that guitar he'd gotten from somewhere.

Eileen was *this close* to stomping across that stage and shutting the whole embarrassing spectacle down. But then the heavyset drummer crashed the cymbals violently and the band stopped short. Bass, guitars, and keys rang out as the metal hiss slowly faded into nothingness. And filling the void… was applause.

Wild, frantic cheers for the band. Cheers for Paul. The other musicians offered exaggerated bows as he slipped out from under the guitar strap and handed the instrument back to the singer. He pressed his hands together humbly and nodded his appreciation to the crowd, then received pats on the back from onlookers while stepping off the stage.

As the next number kicked in, Eileen kept her eye on Paul. He stood as if in a daze, eyes wide but perhaps seeing nothing at all. She felt the tension release from her own body.

Just let him have it. Let him have this moment.

The night that Paul "stole the show," as the media would surely report it. But she knew he would never seize upon this little cameo to get himself back into music seriously. It would, however, perhaps buy her several years' worth of domestic tranquility.

Yes, because Paul Jeffries had finally gotten a taste of glory in the spotlight. He wouldn't trouble Eileen as she moved in for the kill doing the things that *really* mattered in this world.

43. EPILOGUE

Myra Jenkins had her routine set. What trains to take, how long the commute was—and even which cafe near campus made the best coffee.

The first week had been nerve-wracking. Every new thing she'd worried about beforehand had in fact combined to throw her into confusion. But she quickly discovered that everyone at the school was happy to answer her questions about where to go or how to install the student apps on her tablet.

Myra had even made a few friends in the two classes she was taking this semester. Only two because the guidance counselor had suggested she start with a lighter course load to avoid getting overwhelmed. She was fine with that.

Two kids, two classes. Seems about right.

She had also discovered that her fellow undergrads came from many different cultural backgrounds. This immediately put to rest her fears about being the one dark face in a sea of white. Instead, the Regnery School of Art's student body very much looked like New York

City itself. So Myra Jenkins was just one of the many aspiring creators eager to collaborate and learn.

She knew that if she stuck to it through all the challenges that arose, she would one day make everyone proud. Her mother, her kids, her brother Clyde, her man Octavius… and most of all, herself.

It was a nice goal to have.

Marcus Young felt more relaxed now than he had since back in early November, just after he settled in as head of the Modestian medical clinic for military veterans. Otherwise, he would have to go all the way back to the previous spring, right before he was first deployed to go snooping around the Mall of Absolution.

The Jeffries-Lao inauguration had gone off without a hitch, and now the month of January was nearly over. Which meant that warmer weather was right around the corner—and another chance to get back into something he'd neglected for years while out in the field on assignment.

Marcus had a much different field in mind as he entered the Chancellor High School parking lot on this brisk Sunday morning. He pulled on an embroidered FBI cap, then grabbed a dusty oblong bag out of his trunk. The winter air nipped at his bare lower legs as he trotted toward the gymnasium.

He opened the door and was greeted by loud cracks and shouting voices. Someone pointed at him and hollered, "About time! Get over here!"

Marcus grinned and went to shake the man's hand.

"Howdy, Coach. Thanks for the invite. Can't believe I'm finally doing this."

"Team could use a good outfielder. I'm sick of

seeing guys boot routine fly balls, losing us winnable games. But there's no upward age limit in men's league, so what the hell."

"I'll do my best. Just a bit rusty is all."

The coach nodded at Marcus's bag. "How old's that gear?"

"Ah… glove's from the teens, but I did oil it up. Feels great now. As for my bat? Never been used."

Marcus unzipped the narrow pocket at the end of his bag and slid out a pristine wood Louisville Slugger. He smiled.

"Island life, here we come!"

Dawna Jenkins squeezed in between her friends Rita Coleman and Gwen Thomas, who were leaning over the cruise ship railing as it left the Port of Miami.

Rita said, "Bye-bye, USA. Bring on the piña coladas… and the *shopping!*"

As the ladies made their way up a flight of stairs headed for the pool deck bar, Gwen said, "This sure beats fightin' your way through the icy streets of New Jersey. Thank you, Dawna, for being such a generous friend."

"Here, here!" Rita called out. "A nice little getaway for three very vivacious ladies."

The women hugged briefly, then stepped up to the bar. The male server wearing an unbuttoned Hawaiian shirt was dancing to the steel-drum beat of a lively calypso song.

"*Hola, señoritas!* What can I get for you?"

Dawna grabbed Rita's arm and whispered, "He can get that booty moving straight on up to my room, know what I'm sayin'?"

There was laughter and more hugs, until Gwen

finally said to the man, "Baby, c'mere. What's your name... Carlos? Okay, look here. I don't care what you give us, but it's got to be *mixed drinks* only! We got five days on and off this boat. Can't have none of these fine ladies out of commission on account of too many shots."

Carlos bowed. "Your wish is my command. How would you like if I made you one of my personal favorites? It's called, Mango Home With You."

"Ooh, I like the sound of that," Rita said as she threw a hand in the air.

Dawna and friends next settled onto a row of vinyl lounge chairs, each holding a tall plastic aqua cup that was adorned with fruit wedges and an orange umbrella.

She said, "Mrs. Thomas, what if we just stay on this boat forever and leave our troubles behind?"

"I hear that, Dawna darling. I may not be too old for Mister Carlos, but I still am tired."

Rita chirped, "You *can* just lay there. He'll do all the work."

"Nasty! You a nasty lady, Rita."

Dawna looked up at the slowly shifting sky as she said, "I don't know if I can do any more. My boy Clyde, he's hungry. And that friend of mine we was talking about last week, he wants *us* to fight too. But I don't think I got it in me."

Gwen said, "What is this now? You sayin' to forget everything we discussed? No Underground Railroad of the soul? No using our voices to warn of danger, like the drum beats of old?"

Dawna drank through her straw. "Sorry, but I guess not. It's so funny, though. A bright new hat. Stepping off the shore. And one creamy adult libation. That's all it took for me to lose myself. All the weight I been holdin' up? Poof, it's gone. Now I am Island Woman, hear me snore…"

Rita reached out and bumped her cup against Dawna's. "Don't get depressed just 'cause you finally allowed yourself to have a little fun. Now *is* the time to let it all hang out! At least wait til you get back home before deciding if you gonna play hero or not."

"That's exactly right," Gwen said. "Now get on up, the both of you. We got a whole boat to explore. Bars to discover. And men to meet. Let's go!"

Dawna smiled. "You girls really are the best. Thank you for cheering me up. Now, somebody help me out of this chair. I might just poke my head into one of them buffets while we're on the move…"

Eldress Julia Foster stood in front of the dressing table mirror. She looked down at the necklace she had purchased earlier in the day. The fine silver chain felt silky in her palm. Its only ornamentation was a teardrop pearl.

She had just put on a Modestian-approved casual dress which revealed a small area of skin below the neckline. Now she secured the necklace clasp and appraised herself in the mirror.

It was not vanity that told her she looked radiant. Nor was it greed that suggested she might return to the jewelry shop and also buy ball earrings in the same color. No, Julia was only thinking of how to please the man who had noticed *her* among all others—and be worthy of the ultimate honor, should she inhabit the role of Prescient Mistress as Scott Cullen's wife.

Her journey to this moment was singular, but then again, almost every Modestian Julia had spoken to seemed to have a peculiar life story which made them receptive to the new religion.

Her own family had attended a progressive non-denominational church, but even that open-minded sect was not able to satisfy the many clarifications demanded by a child of the "I Totally Exalt Science" generation. If traditional Christian theology could not sufficiently account for the vastness of space, then Julia also wondered why some groups were hesitant, or vehemently opposed, to utilizing inventions and ideas that were possible on this world which God had created for people.

But the supreme paradox to her mind, was how atheists could hold computer logic in such high regard, when according to their beliefs, the universe itself had come about through random and purposeless chance.

She had grappled with these questions privately, as well as with pastors and university professors, but never reached the place of certainty necessary to lead a fully functional life. Then one day, about a year and a half ago, a coworker had forwarded her a short video excerpt from a speech given by the Prescient One. This was intended as a gag to mock the church leader's medieval cloak and feature-obscuring makeup, but the timing coincided with a deep longing for harmony between her mind, body, and soul.

This strange man spoke of striving for balance in life, rather than trying to merge with technology as the solution to human imperfection. He also preached modesty as the ultimate form of empowerment, in an age when flamboyance was seen as the pathway to confidence. Because self-control, he said, protected people against dissipating themselves in wasteful activities, which might trap them in a loop—or even bring about their total destruction.

Within months of first discovering the Modestian gospel, Julia closed up shop on her old life in Missouri and took a leap of faith by moving into the Mall of Absolution. So many of her persistent frustrations simply fell away after she began her half-year trial as a novitiate.

The simple life, one of self-examination and curiosity about one's immediate surroundings... It all proved more manageable, more rewarding, more *intimate* than the lofty aspirations of major religions and scientism alike, which both appeared to overshoot their mark by neglecting the importance of practical daily living.

And now Julia's wildest hopes for a loving future were about to come true, despite how preposterous her conversion to Modestianity had seemed to her family and friends a short while ago. She was ready to aim her own empowered heart like a laser beam at the man adorned in silver and teal, Mr. Scott Cullen.

Mod willing, she would fill the home of this Prescient One with precious little ones in the years to come...

Clyde Jenkins was back at the writing table. For the first time since forever—summer, maybe?—he felt like his mind was in the same place it had been before he uploaded "Fly So High" on a hope and a prayer.

Just his own thoughts now. No rush, no worrying about other people, no hoping the girls would bat their eyes at him. Somehow a lifetime of experiences and wisdom had been crammed into just six months, and tonight he could finally reconnect with himself and explore what he might want to say next.

The new lyrical ideas came fast and in chaotic bursts. Images, themes, and sensory details all poured out onto the page in the same way that his HRA protest song had begun. He wrote about life moving on, estrangement, triumph, disappointment... Of vague wishes turning into reality and the domino effect of consequences...

Waking suddenly in a fancy hotel's king-size bed, after a nightmare which had channeled the real-life moment of violent terror he'd experienced in an alleyway five years ago...

The soundless memory of attending a funeral at a very young age for one of his mother's uncles, the church clothes and somber faces...

Myra coming into his room crying after a loud fight with Dawna—and Clyde too naive to understand what the implications of her being pregnant meant, and why Dawna was so mad...

Lazy summer days spent wandering around the neighborhood with his crew. Convincing the old-timers to give them a sip of beer or a puff of whatever they were smoking out on the stoops...

Discovering new music from anyone and everyone. Straining his ears to identify the singers' unique styles and trying to mimic them note for note. Then thinking that he too would like to be a performer, to live that life on stage...

Delivering a handful of his own rhymes on the corners with friends. Impromptu rap battles during lunch at school, or after a round of basketball at the public courts. Sometimes even hopping up on stage at the local venues, before the serious and more established rappers got going...

Feeling the tingles on the top of his head during those first few days when "Fly So High" started taking off. Dawna and Myra and everyone else screaming themselves silly, crying tears of joy, and embracing each other in the living room of their old apartment...

He would never forget the summer of 'twenty-eight, even if some of the minor moments were lost in the avalanche of new experiences. All the parties, the interviews, the girls, the liquor, the weed…

The dream might have continued on and on and on. But then one day, some *other* group that didn't appreciate the Historical Reparations Administration dropped their own track.

The Sentinels of Jubilee's live broadcast on October seventh had changed the national conversation in an instant—and suddenly Clyde's song was seen in a much more serious light. Everything started to feel tighter, more tense. Instead of friendly Afrigro-American radio hosts, he was talking politics with people who did that sort of thing for a living.

So in hindsight, he couldn't blame himself for changing gears lyrically on his second solo release, "Soul's Gold," which flopped badly. And then he'd recorded the ridiculous song "Ho'Spice" with a couple of accomplished local guys, but that single still wasn't even out yet. Clyde could only guess what Sylicon Smoov and Raw D-Eel were up to at their studio back in the Bronx.

But Clyde had not stopped tumbling forward on his own accelerated track. He eventually gave in to Eddie Pryor's overtures, but only after his mentor Nolan Simmons had made it clear that there was nothing left for him in Newark.

Next arriving in Los Angeles and diving right into work. Soon discovering that *everyone* had something to say to him—whether it was offering life advice, pitching new project ideas, or simply a resounding no.

But he had learned two important things about this town. One, you needed to keep moving forward, and never doubt what had happened in the past. And second, you also had to make time for yourself. To remember who you were, and work on your own passions.

And that's just what Clyde Jenkins was doing right now. Laying the groundwork for solo track number three, after devoting his daytime hours to the collaboration with DJ Low Bought. He would embrace the role of mainstream entertainer, so long as he also got time on the mic to spread his own personal message.

Already he and Eddie had been through enough of the good and the bad, that Clyde could say there was at least one person in all of Los Angeles he could rely on. That was a start.

DJ Clydoscope put his notebook away for the night and looked out the bedroom window. A few stars were peeking through the city's bright glare. He would do everything in his power to keep his own light shining for years to come.

Luis Ortega kicked at some pebbles with his bare feet. A trickle of water eased in and rinsed the sand out from between his toes. Two seagulls cawed as they passed overhead on their journey down the shoreline.

It was breezy but still mostly sunny at the quiet Malibu Lagoon State Beach park. Luis had come here rather than Santa Monica or Venice Beach because he didn't want to be surrounded by noisy tourists. There were only a few dozen other people lounging on the sand or lazily walking around this small cove.

All week he had been stumbling around in a fog. Nothing dramatic had happened. No one else had bothered him at school, either. But without a critical moment to test his newfound resolve, Luis felt like he was bottled up with stress. So he headed to the beach…

He watched some tiny insects rush into a clump of seaweed that was slowly being left behind by the receding tide. His feet made deep prints in the mushy sand, but soon the in-out flows of the cool water washed them all away.

Over to his left, where the lagoon drained out to the ocean, Luis noticed that some people were crossing onto the sandbank from another portion of beach that was closer to Pacific Coast Highway. Curious, he ambled in their direction, until finally realizing that the water level here had dropped to virtually nothing. He also saw that if he kept going south, he'd be able to check out the pier that stood nearby.

As he worked his way up the sandy incline toward the road, some surfers who were paddling around the deeper waters caught his eye. He sat down and watched as they grappled with the choppy waves.

A little while later, one of these guys swam to shore and began heading up the slope with his board tucked under his arm. Luis gave him a thumbs-up.

"Sup, dude?" the surfer said.

"Just chillin', man. Hey, how cold is the water?"

"Ah, you know. Definitely need this!" The surfer slapped at his wetsuit. "But once you get moving, you don't really feel it."

"Cool. Like, how hard is it to do, surfing?"

"You never tried? It's super fun. You should, for sure."

Luis motioned at the surfboard. "But it's got to cost a lot. The gear, right?"

"It *can*. But there's plenty of used stuff out there. The important thing is you get in that ocean. It's special, trust me."

"I think it would be cool. You have lots of friends

that do it?"

"Oh, totally! It's a community, man. A brotherhood. What's your name, by the way?"

"I'm Luis. And you?"

"Colin." They bumped fists. "Good chatting, but I gotta roll here in a minute. You should think about picking up a board, though."

"For real? It's that good?"

"Dude." Colin cast his arm out in the direction of the water. "I'm telling you, man. Once you're out there, everything else goes away. It's just you and the flow. Work *with* it, and you'll catch some great waves right to the shore. But if you fight it… Ha, better cover your head before it tosses you onto the rocks."

"Oh. So it's dangerous then?"

Colin laughed. "It's real life! The danger *and* the thrills. Don't pass it up or you'll miss out. See ya, Lou."

"Later."

Luis turned his attention back to where the other surfers were clustered. He watched them maneuver along the pulsing ocean surface, each waiting for his turn to push up from paddling position and try to catch a brief exhilarating ride, before dropping back into the blue-green sea.

THE END.

ABOUT THE AUTHOR

Originally from Northern Virginia, Philip Wyeth has lived in the Los Angeles area for many years. He's an entrepreneur, musician, film aficionado, hockey fan, and enjoys playing tennis and golf.

Inspired by such unique writers as Heinrich von Kleist, Ambrose Bierce, Joseph Conrad, and Len Deighton, Wyeth's imaginative novels will resonate with fans of Philip K. Dick, Rich Larson, Michel Houellebecq, Bruce Sterling, Barry N. Malzberg, and Neal Stephenson.

Also a lifelong fan of heavy metal music and its many sub-genres, Wyeth strives to infuse his writing with comparable levels of intensity, independence, and larger-than-life visions.

His website is www.philipwyeth.com, and you can follow him across the social media landscape under the following handles:

@PhilipWyeth: Twitter, BitChute, Gab, and Minds.

@PhilipWyethWriter: Instagram and Facebook.

www.ingramcontent.com/pod-product-compliance
Lightning Source LLC
Chambersburg PA
CBHW051923110726
47902CB00002B/390